POISON IN PADDINGTON

CASSIE COBURN MYSTERY #1

SAMANTHA SILVER

BLUEBERRY BOOKS PRESS

I could only remember bits and pieces from the night that changed my life forever. I remembered headlights. Everything in front of me had been dark; I'd left the hospital where I was doing my residency just after two am. Then, suddenly, everything in the parking lot I'd been walking through was illuminated. Funnily enough, I remembered perfectly that the car directly in front of me was a white BMW three-series. What I didn't remember was the red Toyota Camry whose lights shone onto it smashing into my left side.

The next thing I remembered, I was being taken into the hospital on a stretcher. It had been almost like an out-of-body experience. I'd already spent so much of my life in that hospital. I was completing my residency there. I'd gone there so many times for classes while still in medical school. But each of those times, I'd walked through the doors. This time, however, I was being carted in, like I'd seen happen to so many people before me.

Kirsten, one of the nurses, was crying, her tears flowing freely down her cheeks. She was still able to bark out orders though, yelling for the emergency doctor on call that night, Doctor Evans, to come straight away. Just two hours earlier, I'd been congratulating her on her engagement to a local firefighter.

I stared at the ceiling tiles as I was carted down the hallway. I don't remember being in any pain, oddly enough. Maybe my brain had repressed that part of it. Given the path we were going, I instantly knew where I was being taken. The operating room. Apparently my tibia was sticking out of my leg. You didn't exactly need twelve years of medical training to know that was going to need surgery. The irony was, I was training to be an orthopedic surgeon. The doctor I'd followed on rounds just that morning would be the one stitching my ACL back together and putting a metal rod in my leg.

And the true tragedy was, if it had just been my leg, everything would have been fine. I was obviously going to have to go through months of rehab, but in the end I'd be able to walk again. I'd be able to live my life normally, and start my career as a surgeon—a career that I'd spent almost half my life working toward.

When I woke up from surgery, my leg was in a cast. But more importantly, so was my hand. It was discovered after the emergency surgery on my leg that I'd also broken four phalanges, the metacarpal bone in my thumb, and four other bones in my hand, as well as having torn two tendons in my wrist.

And just like that, my career as a surgeon was over. It felt like my life was over, too.

I slowly learned more about what had happened to me. The man who had hit me was high; he had come to the hospital so he could try to get more narcotics. To be honest, I didn't really care. When Kirsten came in and explained to me what had happened, I'd just stared at the wall. I didn't feel anything. I didn't cry. I didn't scream. I was just numb. After all, what did it matter? What did it matter if he was high, or drunk, or completely sober? It didn't change the facts. I was never going to be a surgeon. Hell, I was probably never going to be a doctor. Sure, I could work as a GP. I could write sick notes for people with the sniffles. I could order blood tests before sending people off to see the kind of doctor I was supposed to be. That wasn't what I'd wanted. That wasn't supposed to be the way my life turned out.

My mom kept telling me how lucky I was. How I could have died. And, I supposed she was right, in a way. If you're going to get hit by a car, you might as well get hit fifty feet from the emergency doors to a hospital, right? Plus, the fact that he was driving in a parking lot meant that he wasn't going *that* fast. The fact that it was a Camry and not a Ferrari helped, too.

But the more she, and everyone else, kept telling me that, the unluckier I felt. Wouldn't it have been better if I'd just died? After all, what was the point in living now? I'd spent my whole life working to be a surgeon. I'd been in school for twenty-five of my thirty years. I had graduated from college. I had finished medical school. I had completed four and a half years of my residency. I was a mere six months away from officially being a practicing doctor, instead of just a resident. And now, all that was gone.

Each night, before I fell asleep, I wondered if things wouldn't be better if I just didn't wake up the next morning.

CHAPTER 1

The weather in London that morning was absolutely perfect. It was an early spring day in late March, the sun was shining but there was still a crisp bite to the air that made me glad I'd decided to throw on a light jacket before I'd gone out. I'd also remembered to throw my new mini umbrella in my purse before I left. I'd only been living in London for a week, but I'd already learned the importance of carrying an umbrella around at all times—no matter how deceiving the sky looked.

Let me go back a little bit. My name is Cassie Coburn, and I'm almost thirty-one years old. I moved to London a week ago in a last-ditch attempt to get over the crippling depression I'd been suffering from ever since getting hit by a car ten months ago.

In the end, I had a broken leg, a torn ACL, and I'd broken enough bones and torn enough tendons in my hand to lose 5 percent use of it. Now, for most people, that wouldn't mean anything. Five percent use of your hand means you occasionally drop your fork when you try to pick it up. The problem was, I was trained as an orthopedic surgeon. And at twenty-nine, with a job offer on the table and a career I'd worked toward my entire adult life up to that point, it had all been taken away.

I could no longer work as a surgeon. I wasn't safe. Even if I thought it was fine – and I wasn't about to risk someone else's limbs because *I* thought I felt ok - no one would insure me. I fell into a crippling depression, a black hole that I couldn't get out of. Not that I'd made much of an effort to try.

My mom, being my mom, made sure to get a lawyer who sued the impaired driver to oblivion and back. Future earnings, and all that. A month ago I'd received a check for about ten million dollars in damages from his insurance company. It was meant to compensate me for the money I would have earned in a lifetime as a surgeon. The money didn't make me happy though. Nothing made me happy anymore.

Finally, on an impulse, I had decided to do something I'd never done before in an attempt to gain control over my life once more. I booked a flight to London leaving the next day. My dad was Scottish; even though he'd moved to America when he was a kid, he'd made sure I'd gotten my UK passport when I was born, so there were no visa issues. I called my mom and told her I was leaving. She was actually amazingly understanding. My mom was normally the overprotective, neurotic type, and I thought that telling her I was flying to the other side of the world with no idea what I was going to do would drive her over the edge. Instead, she wished me luck and told me to take all the time I needed.

That was when I'd known I was making the right call. When *my mom,* of all people, thought me doing something impulsive and crazy was a good idea, it meant I was not in a good place here.

And as it turned out, so far, this had actually been a good idea! I was staying at a hostel downtown until I found somewhere permanent to live. Having been a student for so long I knew how to live pretty frugally. I wasn't about to spend a couple grand a night staying at the Ritz. All the little things that I'd taken for granted in San Francisco: having a bank account, knowing where to get the cheapest groceries, the best place for takeout at any hour of the day, that sort of thing—were all things I had to rediscover. And they forced me out of my bed. After all, if I just stayed in my bed in the hostel all day, I was eventually going to starve.

Even the almost-constant rain made me feel happy, since it was so different to what I'd grown up with in San Francisco. But, as I was to discover that morning, not everything was perfectly rosy in Jolly Ol' England.

I skipped out the front door of the hostel,

7

thinking that I might wander around, try the kebab place down the street for lunch that I'd heard a couple of Canadians raving about the night before, and then take my bike over to the London Eye and do a bit of sightseeing. One of the first things I had done when I'd gotten here was to hit up Gumtree—basically the UK version of Craigslist—where I'd found a lady selling a cheap bike. It was one of those cruiser bikes, painted in a beautiful turquoise blue. Sure, it had a couple of dents here and there, and there was a tear on the seat, but it was perfect for getting around the city, and she'd only wanted twenty pounds for it. Sold!

I knew the underground was an essential part of London life. But honestly, to start with, I just wanted to explore the city. I'd never really been outside of San Francisco before. My mom was single, and had done her best, but we hadn't had much money for traveling when we were young. And of course, once I'd started medical school, even if I had wanted to travel I couldn't afford the time *or* the money. Besides, this was *London*! This was one of the most popular, most incredible, most historically rich cities in the world. It seemed like every time I turned the corner I found myself standing somewhere where important historical events had taken place. I was determined to truly see the city, not just travel underneath it to get from place to place.

Of course, it turned out that London was absolutely not bicyclist friendly. But I didn't know that at the time, and I'd become a little bit attached to my bike, even though I mainly just rode it—extremely carefully—down the less busy streets, and walked it along the sidewalk the rest of the time.

So imagine my surprise that morning when I left the hostel and went down the side alley to where I locked up my bike every night against a pole announcing no parking, only to find the lock had been cut through, abandoned on the concrete, my bike nowhere to be seen.

"Aw, you have *got* to be kidding me," I said, frustration making its way through me. Less than a week and I had already fallen victim to a theft. At least it wasn't like the bike had cost a ton of money, but still! It was the principle of the thing, and I liked that bike. It was pretty.

I looked around the alley for a bit, as if there was any chance that my bike had broken its own lock and just moved around about thirty feet, or that someone broke the lock and then had a change of heart a minute later and left it behind the dumpster that was halfway down the alley. Unfortunately, there was no such luck. I sighed and took out my phone. On my first day here I'd made sure to grab a UK SIM card, and I was now loaded up with tons of free text, talking minutes and data that made me feel incredibly self-conscious about the fact that I had exactly zero contacts in my phone so far. Still, the data was incredibly handy for finding things when I was out.

I discovered the closest police station was right by

the nearest tube station, at Edgware Road. I typed the address into my Google Maps app and made my way over there. After all, if I had any chance of getting my bike back in this new city, it was going to have to be with the help of the cops.

CHAPTER 2

The Edgware Road Police Station, listed as part of the Metropolitan Police Service, fit in with the rest of the neighborhood, a strange juxtaposition of old buildings with interesting architecture, and dirty metal structures obviously built in the seventies and eighties. Falling into the latter category, the exterior of the building was nothing special. Concrete was featured heavily in the construction of the building, and the glass around it was tinted, giving the whole thing an especially dirty look. A uniformed policeman stood outside, briefly ensuring that anyone entering the building was actually there on police business.

I cautiously made my way toward the man.

"Hi, am I in the right place to report a stolen bike?" I asked nervously, and he smiled at me kindly.

"Yes, you are, absolutely. Please take the stairs to

the third floor. Unfortunately, the lift is broken today and the repairman isn't coming in until later today."

"Thanks," I said, moving past him and entering the building. The hustle and bustle inside was in stark comparison to the calm outside. Everywhere I looked, there were uniformed officers and people wearing civilian clothes moving around efficiently, and I quickly felt like perhaps in the whole scheme of maintaining law and order in this neighborhood of London, perhaps a stolen bicycle was a waste of time. Still, I was here now, and the man outside hadn't seemed perturbed by the relative insignificance of the crime I had fallen victim to.

I steeled myself and found the staircase, making my way up. I smiled to myself when I didn't feel any pain in my knee. Despite my depression, Kirsten had made sure I always went to my physiotherapy appointments. While I walked with a very slight limp, a couple of flights of stairs here and there no longer gave me any trouble. Two flights of stairs later, I found myself in the middle of an open floor plan filled with plain clothed people and the odd uniformed officer moving around. There was no reception desk, and no indication of where I should go to file a report.

Coming toward me, was a man and woman who both seemed to be around my age. They couldn't have possibly looked more different. He wore a fancy suit, the dark blue of which went well with his light red hair and freckles that covered his friendly-looking face. Carrying a handful of files, he looked all business, but his face still had that kindness that made me think he was a good person. He was the type of policeman you wanted to see on the street, the kind of man that gave the impression that he would keep you safe, but also wouldn't be overly aggressive if he caught you smoking a joint. She, on the other hand, had long, chestnut brown hair tied back into a ponytail, skinny jeans and a long boho top. A pair of huge sunglasses sat on top of her head, and she was wearing flip flops. Flip flops! She couldn't have been a cop. Absolutely no way. But him? Definitely. It was worth a shot, anyway.

"Excuse me?" I tried, going up to the two of them. The woman stopped and gave me a look as if she was surprised that I would dare interrupt them, but the look on his face was one of polite curiosity. I decided to address myself to him, and continued.

"I was directed here to report a stolen bike, but I'm afraid I don't know exactly who I should speak to. Could you help me?"

The man smiled, and the girl next to him smirked. "Of course. Listen, I can take care of this for you, why don't you follow me into this room here?" he asked. He started walking to the left of where we were standing, where I saw a number of small conference rooms lining the wall.

"Seriously?" I heard the woman ask him. "You have got to be kidding me." She had a French accent, and a strong one at that.

"We don't pay you to help us out, you can always leave," he told her.

"We both know you don't have a chance in hell of solving this case if I do," she replied, and I couldn't help but wonder what they were talking about.

"We have been known to solve cases before without your help."

"Not ones like this."

The man opened the door to one of the conference rooms and motioned for me to sit down at the desk. I did so, suddenly feeling like perhaps this had been a bad idea.

The conference room had a whiteboard against one side, with the chemical formula for strychnine, a poison, written on it. There was a small table in the middle, large enough to seat eight people, with that many chairs around it. I sat down at one and fiddled with my hands, and the man sat in one of the chairs on the other side. I couldn't help but feel a little bit uncomfortable, like I'd wandered into something way bigger than a stolen bike, and that I maybe should have just sucked up the loss. After all, it sounded like there was serious police work being done here. The woman moved to the corner and stood there, watching us. I couldn't help but get the feeling that she was studying me, and it gave me the creeps. The weirdest part about it was that she didn't hide it. She just straight up stared me down while the other guy took a notebook out of his pocket and began asking me questions.

"I'm DCI Tony Williams. Now, you said you had a missing bicycle? Where was it locked up?"

"Against a pole in an alley next to the hostel I was staying at," I said, giving him all the details I had about the bike – the color, what I'd paid for it, that sort of thing.

"When did you see the bike last?"

"When I locked it up last night around six."

He jotted the info down in his notebook and asked a few more questions.

"Right. Now I'll just take down some basic information about you and we can be out of here."

The woman interrupted then, her French accent somehow making her sound even more superior than her demeanour already was.

"She's an American, recently moved to London. A doctor, but she doesn't practice, probably because of the accident she was in. She grew up relatively poor, but has come into money recently. She has a bit of a desire to be adventurous, but her conservative upbringing has limited the amount of risk she's willing to take."

"Thank you, Violet," DCI Williams said with a small smile, "but I was thinking more along the lines of her phone number."

"Oh I know, I just wanted to see the look," the girl named Violet replied with a small smile. I didn't even need to ask what look she was talking about; I knew it was exactly the one I was doing now. My mouth

15

hung open, my eyes wide, shocked that she knew all these things.

"How could you *possibly* know that?" Violet stepped out of the corner, a small smile on her face.

"Your accent gives away that you're American. Your clothes are all American brands so you haven't lived in London long enough to need to replace any of them. Plus, you came to the second floor rather than the third floor where you were directed, forgetting that we have a ground floor in Europe."

My face flushed red as I realized she was right; I'd completely forgotten about the whole ground floor thing. But before I had a chance to be too embarrassed, she continued. "When you saw the formula written on the white board, you didn't just look at it, you *read* it. So you're trained in chemistry, but you don't have the hands of a chemist; you're actually wearing nail polish, and you don't have any scars or traces of experiments gone wrong. So you're a doctor. But you've been in an accident, it's obvious from the way you walk that your left knee is out of joint, and when you were fiddling with your hands I noticed a slight delay in the reaction from your left hand as well. That says stroke, or accident. For a healthy looking young woman like you, the odds are in favor of an accident. An accident, in America, and traveling relatively soon afterwards? You sued and you won. But you grew up poor because despite the fact that I imagine you're now incredibly well off, you still came to the police station to report a thirty-pound bike being stolen."

I didn't think it was possible, but my mouth dropped open even more.

"That's incredible!" I practically whispered. If I wasn't mistaken, Violet actually smiled.

"Most people accuse me of stalking them."

"No. No, your logic, it's perfect. It's just…"

"No one thinks logically, so when I do it, it's impressive."

"Something like that. But how did you decide that I wish I was adventurous, but limit the risks I take?"

"You decided to move halfway around the world, which was an adventurous move on its own, but you also came to England, rather than going somewhere exotic. Adventurous, but you made sure to stay somewhere where the language is the same as yours and you're not going to experience too much culture shock."

"They would have burned you at the stake a couple hundred years ago."

There was that small smile again. "Yes, it's rather fortunate that we live in such an enlightened age. Although some of DCI Williams' colleagues here would have preferred us to stay in the Middle Ages."

DCI Williams shifted uncomfortably in his chair. "Yes, well, you help us find the serial killer, Violet, and I'll make sure everyone knows it was all thanks to you."

She waved him away. "You know I do not want

the thanks. I simply see it as my civic duty to solve the crimes. It is simply because so many of your colleagues are *imbéciles* that I manage it so much better."

DCI Williams stood up. "Thanks for coming in, Miss Coburn. Don't worry about getting the wrong floor; I'll make sure the right people get these notes. And sorry about…" he trailed off, his head tilting slightly toward Violet.

"Do you really think, Detective Chief Inspector Williams, that I do not know that you're apologizing about me? Do you think so little of me that you think that's fooling me?" Violet asked. "No matter. Take out the files, we can get on with the important stuff now," she urged. I knew I should have been insulted at that, but somehow, I couldn't be. This Violet, I didn't know who she was, but she was different, that was for sure. I thanked them both and left the way I came, wondering about the strange Frenchwoman who seemed to know everything about me, while all I knew about her was her first name.

CHAPTER 3

To be honest, I never expected to hear back from the cops. After all, what was a thirty pound bike compared to all the big crimes that must be happening in London on a daily basis? That Violet woman had practically told me my crime wasn't even worth paying any attention to. And I couldn't really argue with that, quite frankly.

The German girl I was sharing a room with had gone out to a club, and I'd briefly perused the internet on my iPad, looking for a place to live permanently. Unfortunately, what I hadn't realized was that the housing market in London was just as crazy as in San Francisco. Everything that was in a price range I wanted to consider either involved having eight roommates, sharing the space with a copious number of rats going by the droppings I saw in the picture, non-functioning plumbing—one place had an outhouse! An actual outhouse!—, or living in a space where the double bed took up over half the living space.

I was just about to start wondering if maybe I should up my budget a little bit—after all, it wasn't like I was wanting for money anymore, but I also didn't want to be wasteful while I didn't have a job—when my phone began to ring. At first, I had no idea what the sound even was. After all, it wasn't like I had this thriving social life with people calling me at all hours of the day. I realized how sad it was that I barely recognized my own ringtone, and realized the caller was probably going to be a telemarketer, but it was a phone call all the same!

Thinking that maybe this was a whole new low, I pressed the answer button and half-heartedly said hello to the worker bee on the other side.

"'Allo? This is Cassie Coburn?" came a familiar French accent on the other side.

"Uh… yes, yeah it is," I said. Violet's voice was the last I had expected to hear.

"Come to my place. Eighteen Eldon Road, Kensington."

Before I had a chance to reply, she had hung up the phone. I took mine away from my ear and stared at it. Seriously?

When did she want me to come over? Now? What for? Was she going to kidnap me and torture me in her basement? I mean, she was super skinny, but with my injured knee I wasn't totally sure I could take her if she tried. And honestly, she gave off a bit of a vibe that meant I wasn't sure my body wasn't going to end up being found mutilated in the Thames.

But also, a part of me was intrigued. I couldn't help but remember what she'd said that afternoon: that I wanted excitement, but I wasn't a risk taker. This wasn't even that big a risk.

Before I could change my mind, I got up, grabbed my purse and opened up Google Maps to see how to get to Kensington.

Forty-five minutes later—I had gotten on the wrong underground line the first time around and had to double back—I was standing in front of a townhouse with a gorgeous façade. It was an off-white, with that late Georgian look to it that just screamed class. Walking cautiously up to the front door, I steeled myself for whatever was going to come next, and knocked three times.

My heart was pounding through my chest as I waited. About a minute later the front door opened.

"Got lost, did you?" Violet said with a hint of a smile.

"Just a little bit," I muttered, blushing.

"I'm teasing you, but you cannot expect Americans to know how to read a tube map. You have nothing remotely resembling decent transit."

It wasn't like the BART system was the world's greatest, but I still felt a little bit insulted. Before I had a chance to retort, however, Violet led me into the house and straight into an old-style living room. The far wall was lined with a giant bookshelf from floor to ceiling, every inch of it taken. The hardwood floors creaked slightly underfoot, and the dim lamp lighting gave the whole place a classy, old-world kind of look. A comfortable-looking couch was shoved away in the corner, and a table on the other side of the room was covered in papers.

I barely noticed any of that, however. My sight was fixed on my turquoise bike, sitting in the middle of the room, as if on a pedestal.

"My bike!" I cried out, rushing over to it and running my hands over it, like I had to touch it to believe it was real. "Thank you!" I said, looking over at Violet, who waved my thanks away.

"It was nothing. I needed a palate cleanser this afternoon. There's something off about my case and I hoped finding a petty criminal would distract me for a while."

I had no idea what she was talking about. "Did it work?" I asked.

"No. I am no closer to solving the case."

"Well thank you for my bike. How did you do it?"

Violet did that little smile again. "It will stop being impressive if I tell you *all* my secrets."

I looked over at the desk with all those papers. One of them stood out to me, the chemical symbol for strychnine, same as I'd seen that morning at the police station. Almost instinctively, I got up and went over and had a look. Sure enough, that was what it was. Some sort of lab report, by the looks.

"Strychnine. You had a poisoning victim," I said.

"I had four poisoning victims," Violet replied. "All of them with strychnine. You Americans. You always feel like you have the right to go anywhere," she told me, leaning casually against the doorframe.

"Oh, sorry," I blushed, realizing that I had really just gone into her private things. But instead of getting mad, Violet waved away my apology.

"You are a doctor, tell me what you think. Four people were poisoned with strychnine yesterday afternoon, at a soup stall in Paddington."

I tried to remember everything I could about strychnine.

"Strychnine is a paralytic. If I remember correctly, it takes few minutes before the symptoms start, and it's a crazy painful way to die."

I stopped, but Violet didn't say anything else, so I continued. "It's got a bitter taste, though. And with a small dosage, since it usually takes a few hours to die and we're in central London, all a person would have to do would be to go to the hospital. They'd probably give them activated charcoal to absorb anything they could, and so without having ingested a large dose, chances are the victim would survive. But a large dose would mean the strychnine would be tasted."

Violet nodded this time. "Good. That is what happened. The soup cart owner served four people from that particular pot. When numbers three and four both complained that the soup was bitter, she assumed that the kitchen had screwed it up and stopped serving it."

"But anyone who's done even a tiny bit of research would know strychnine is bitter. If you're trying to poison as many people as possible, then you would want to go as long as possible without being noticed."

Violet's eyes lit up. "Yes. Exactly. Keep going."

I could feel my brain trying to make connections, trying to get to the point Violet wanted me to figure out, but I couldn't quite get there.

"So your serial killer is either incredibly stupid, which seems unlikely but probably also not unheard of," I muttered, then it came to me. "Oh!" I continued, my eyes widening. "I know! Strychnine is painful. It's a terrible way to die. You would only use it on your worst enemy, or someone you're trying to murder. It wasn't a serial killer, it was someone who wanted the police to think they were a serial killer, but who was really out to kill only one person!"

Violet grinned, and I couldn't help but notice that when she really smiled she was incredibly beautiful.

"Excellent. You are smarter than the entire London police force. I told them that this afternoon, of course, but no. They think the killer wanted to hurt random people. Obviously not. As you say, only a moron would use strychnine. And there are a lot of morons who kill people, but this is not one of them."

"So what do you do now? When the police don't believe you, I mean?" I was curious, and more than just a little bit intrigued. It had been quite a while since I'd actually had to use my brain, and like the first time I got to exercise after my accident, I found that I'd missed it.

Violet shrugged. "I solve the crime. I hand them their killer on a silver platter. And then they thank me, and they wonder why they cannot solve the crime on their own. I tell them it is because they do not think, and they are insulted. And the next interesting case comes around, and they do the same thing."

"But you don't work for the police?" I asked, and she laughed, a soft, mocking laugh.

"*Mon dieu,* no. What an idea, that one. I help the police out of civic duty. And because occasionally they have a case that's interesting enough to be worth my time. This case, this one is interesting. We have a person who wants to murder someone. That is fine, it happens all the time. But they are willing to murder other people as well, innocent people, and pretend to be a serial killer to cover their tracks? Now that, that is interesting."

"So what are you going to do now?" I asked.

"What do you think I'm going to do?" Violet replied. I wanted to throw up my hands in frustration. I didn't know! I wasn't the detective! Still, I thought about it for a few seconds.

"Now you have to sort through the victims and see which one was the person who was supposed to be killed, and find out who killed them."

"*Exactement!* The first step is see who was supposed to be killed today. Good! Very good!" She clapped her hands together, obviously happy with my deduction. She picked up four file folders and handed them to me.

"Take these with you. Read them tonight. They are the people who were killed. Then, in the morning, you will come back here. We will go and find out who was killed on purpose, and who was killed by accident."

I took the files, filled with conflicting feelings of confusion and excitement. Was I honestly being invited to help Violet out with her murder investigation?

"But… why?" I asked. "Why me?"

"Because you are depressed and you need something to do. And I need someone to talk to who will occasionally answer back with something more intelligent than the babble of DCI Williams. And he's the best of the lot. I should tell you though, I'm not the easiest person to work with."

"I'd gathered that," I replied, trying to hide a smile.

"Good. So you will come tomorrow." It was more statement than question.

A part of me was tempted to say no. After all, I had a big day of doing absolutely nothing planned for the following day, just like most days in the past ten months. But another part of me was intrigued. A little bit about the case, yes. But more about Violet. She was an interesting person; unlike anyone I'd ever met before.

And that, more than anything, was why I eventually answered "yeah, sure, why not?"

I left the house with the files, and my bike, and slowly made my way back home. I couldn't help but wonder what on earth I'd just gotten myself into.

CHAPTER 4

*B*y the time I got back to my hostel, I was almost wondering if I hadn't dreamt everything. Violet gave off that kind of impression, like she wasn't quite real. But the bike in my hand and the files I was holding proved otherwise.

Realizing I didn't have a lock for my bike anymore, I snuck it in past the reception area while the bored-looking guy from Australia ducked into the back for a minute, and stored it in my room. I knew my roommate wouldn't mind at all, and I made a mental note to get a new bike lock in the morning. I knew I should probably sell the bike, since London wasn't exactly cyclist-friendly, but I liked it. It was the first real thing I'd bought in England, and I'd become attached to it.

That probably wasn't exactly healthy.

Pushing that thought to the back of my brain— my long term mental health was a problem for

Future Cassie to deal with—I grabbed the files and sat down on my bed. Opening the first one, I saw it was a full police file. There was a five by seven-inch corporate headshot of a man who looked to be in his early thirties. He was just starting to go bald, and had that deer-in-headlights look that wasn't exactly flattering.

Putting the photo to one side, I read the report behind it. Some of it was stuff I already knew. Manner of death: poison – strychnine. Time of death: 13:42. Location of murder: Sandy's Stews, Paddington, London. Then below was a lot of personal information. The man's name, for one. Stephen Glastonbury. He had lived in Chelsea and worked for a financial firm as a broker. He'd been meeting a client in Paddington, hence his reason for being in that part of the city.

I scanned the rest of the document, then grabbed the next one. Elizabeth Dalton, a woman in her fifties who had her hair pulled back into a bun on the back of her head. She had lived and worked in Paddington, as a secretary to the head of marketing at a major insurance company. Enderby Insurance. The name was familiar; I was fairly certain I'd seen a number of their ads around town. They must have been a huge company. Elizabeth Dalton's commute was less than ten minutes on foot, I noted when I saw her address, looking up Crawford Road on my phone. Not too shabby, I thought to myself as I flipped over to the next folder. I'd heard the horror stories of people commuting for hours to get to their jobs in the city. Looking at the map of London, the suburbs seemed to extend all the way to the English Channel. Of course, there was a chance that had she worked literally anywhere else she'd still be alive right now, and the thought made me a little bit sad.

The next folder featured a man in his early forties who could be considered in shape—if you considered round a shape, that was. Pietro Murillo, an immigrant from Italy who ran an importing business, was visiting a potential customer in the neighborhood. He lived in Brixton, and I couldn't help but smile at the line that read "Known health conditions: none", where someone who must have been Violet scratched it out and wrote "WRONG—GRAVES DISEASE" in a fat red pen. I took a closer look at the photo. Sure enough, the telltale sign was there. Jonathan Murillo's eyes bulged only slightly, but enough for it to be noticeable if you knew what to look for, and although the lighting for the headshot was quite frankly pretty terrible, I was fairly certain his eyelids were red and puffy as well. So Violet knew quite a bit about medicine herself. Somehow, I wasn't surprised.

I opened up the last folder, that of a woman in her early twenties who worked at a fast food restaurant down the street from the square where the soup cart had been. I made a mental note to never eat there; if she—while on minimum wage—was willing to forgo the free food that was available for her to eat at her workplace to go buy soup from a cart, there was no way I was going to trust what came out of that kitchen. Her name was Sally Abbott, and she lived somewhere in East London, I had to look up the suburb name on my phone as I didn't recognize it.

I found myself poring over the files, trying to figure out which one of these four had been the intended target, and which three were unfortunate victims. But much to my chagrin, as more time passed, the further I got from figuring out anything from the basic biographical information I'd been given about the victims. Eventually, I realized three hours had passed, and that if I wanted to be even remotely presentable the next day when I went murderer hunting for the first time, I had probably better get some sleep.

I put the files under my mattress just in case, then slipped into my pyjamas and went to bed, wondering what my first day helping out a detective who didn't work with the police, but who seemed to know what she was doing all the same, was going to bring.

As MY EYES opened up the next morning, I was vaguely aware of a shape sitting on the edge of my bed. Fearing a robber, I let out a squeal and quickly sat up.

"With reflexes like that you're a prime target for a serial killer," Violet said as she casually flipped through the files that I was sure I'd left under my mattress. "I've been sitting here for twenty minutes."

My body was a mixture of confusion, anger, and the grogginess that can only come from not being fully awake. While I meant to ask Violet how the hell she got into my apartment, the question actually came out as a very elegant "how you in?" as I tried to wipe the sleep from my eyes.

"Please. This is a central London youth hostel; it is not exactly the Barclay's vault. Besides, I said I would see you in the morning. We have work to do."

"I believe you said you'd *call* me in the morning, not that I'd wake up finding you sitting on the edge of my bed like some kind of crazy person."

"*Bien*, things change. You looked at these files last night?" I nodded in response. "Good. Then get up, and get changed. We have time to get breakfast, then we have to visit the two people who were the potential targets."

"Two?" I asked. "But there are four folders."

Violet's mouth crept up into that little enigmatic smile again. "There are. And if you had read them carefully, you would know there was no way two of the people could have been murdered there on purpose."

I leaned my head back against the wall. "How? I spent hours looking at those files last night. I have all the basic information memorized. Good call on the Graves disease, by the way."

"Ah, you liked that, did you? I thought you might. Get dressed, I will explain as we have breakfast."

Fifteen minutes later I'd thrown on a pair of black yoga pants and the only blouse I had brought to London, thinking that maybe I should look professional, even though today Violet was wearing a flowing turquoise skirt that reached her knees and a black top spattered with rainbow-coloured pot leaves. I imagined DCI Williams wouldn't exactly approve.

"There is an excellent breakfast spot just down the street from the square where the murder took place," Violet told me, leading the way. To be honest, I was totally down for a bacon and egg McMuffin and a couple hash browns, or whatever the British equivalent was. I certainly wasn't expecting to be taken to an organic fair-trade, gluten-free, lactose-free, refined-sugar-free vegan café that smelled like ginger, eucalyptus oil and coffee beans.

"Is this... what you eat?" I asked Violet carefully, eyeing the quinoa granola bars with caution. The girl behind the counter looked like she'd come straight out of the sixties, and the barista had a hipster beard and looked like he belonged on the cover of an alternative music magazine.

"Of course," she replied. "The brain is my most valuable tool. As a doctor, you always keep your equipment in prime condition. I have to do the same. As should you, your brain is as important as your scalpel, in your profession."

"I'm not a doctor anymore," I said lamely.

"You are always going to be a doctor, no matter what job you have," Violet replied as she perused the menu. She ordered a bowl of almond mylk—yes, it said mylk—soaked overnight oats with organic honey and berries, topped with flax and chia seeds, as well as bee pollen. Really? Bee pollen? Those were not words I ever thought I'd see on a restaurant menu. I looked at the menu. I knew all the words described foods, but I had never seen them in that order before.

I had been a student for so long, my diet generally consisted of fast and cheap. I could order my way through a kebab shop or tell you which brand of ramen noodles tasted best, but this was just all new territory for me.

Finally, I settled on the most normal looking stuff on the menu: a red fruit smoothie—made with almond mylk, of course—and waffles. Waffles were normal, right?

Of course, it turned out they were made with bananas and oat flour instead of normal flour, and topped with goji berries, chia seeds, coconut flakes, something called cashew cream that I carefully avoided, but thankfully also maple syrup.

Violet watched me with an amused smile on her face as I carefully crafted my plate around which foods I was going to eat, and which ones I was going to ignore.

"You know," she finally said. "If you actually try eating it, you might be pleasantly surprised."

No, I thought to myself, I was definitely going to keep acting like a two-year-old who decided they didn't like food without trying it. After all, I didn't need to try the cashew cream to know I wasn't going to like it. Just look at the name, for goodness' sake!

I eventually took a bite, and to my surprise, I actually enjoyed the waffle. The smoothie was delicious as well, nice and smooth. The cashew cream was disgusting, but I pretended not to mind it, just to impress Violet. I couldn't believe I was doing it, I felt like a little girl trying to impress her older sister, but I was fairly certain Violet and I were around the same age. She just seemed so... confident. She seemed like she had everything together. Like she, unlike me, was absolutely nailing this whole being-an-adult thing.

"Good," Violet finally said. "Now that you have decided to eat like an adult for what appears to be the first time in your life, shall we discuss the case?"

I looked suitably embarrassed at my complete and total lack of ability to order food in a health food restaurant, but as I dug into my waffles and kept drinking my smoothie, we started discussing the case.

"So how do you know that there are only two people who could be the target?" I asked through a bit of waffle. "And which two are they?"

"You need to *think*, that is why you did not figure

it out. You saw the words, but you did not think about what they mean. Why was everyone at the square that morning?"

"One guy was meeting a client, one was meeting a customer and two were working."

"*Exactement!*"

"Ohhhhhh," I exclaimed, my eyes widening as I made the connection. "Of course!" Violet broke out into a big smile as I figured it out. "The two that weren't regulars, there was no way the killer could have known where they were going to have lunch."

"*Ah, parfait!*" Violet exclaimed, evidently pleased. "I did not think you would realize it on your own. You are better than most, at thinking."

I blushed slightly at the praise. "So that means either Elizabeth Dalton or Sally Abbott was the intended victim. Now, we have to figure out which one of those two someone wanted dead."

"Ah, but that, I have already figured out," Violet said. "Sally Abbott worked in a casual role, at a restaurant. She would have different hours for her break depending on how busy they were on any given day. The killer would have had to know more or less when she was going to go on break, to know when to poison the stew. After all, the killer would have known that the taste would be noticed. He—I only use the male pronoun for simplicity's sake, it could very well be a woman—would have wanted to poison the soup as close to the lunch break of the victim as possible. Elizabeth Dalton worked as a secretary at an insurance company. She would have taken her break at the same time every single day, so as to not upset the routine of the office. The killer would have known this, and been able to slip the poison into the stew just before she went on break."

I looked at Violet with a combination of exasperation and awe. She had figured that out just from the regular police report outlining the most basic facets of a person's existence. It was incredibly impressive, but I also wondered what on earth we were doing here then.

"Well then why are we here?" I asked. "If you already know."

"I made an appointment to meet with Elizabeth Dalton's boss. I want to look through her things before the police get around to it and ruin it all. You have ten minutes to finish eating your waffles."

"Aren't you going to tell the police what you know?"

"I've already told them. They still believe it was a random serial killer. DCI Williams will eventually come around to my way of thinking; he is smarter than the others. But for now he can chase his ghost, and we get the opportunity to do some investigation without the police getting in the way."

I had to smile at Violet's calm air of arrogance. It suited her somehow, the way she didn't say it to be boastful, she just said it as, well, a fact. And to be honest, I was hard pressed to disagree with what I'd seen so far. Everything she'd said up until now had made perfect sense.

Finishing up my waffles and smoothie, I had to admit that perhaps the vegan food wasn't as scary as I thought. I also secretly promised myself though that I'd get the greasiest slice of pizza I could find for lunch. Then, the two of us made our way to the offices of Enderby Insurance.

Their offices were on the tenth, eleventh and twelfth floors of a large glass tower that screamed modern. Violet introduced us to the guard at the bottom of the tower, who eyed her shirt with a look of distrust, but eventually let us through to the elevators where we made our way upstairs. I was about to be involved in my first murder mystery interview. Despite myself, I was actually a little bit excited. And scared. Definitely scared. After all, what if we were about to meet someone who was secretly a murderer? As the high-speed elevator rushed us up to the twelfth floor, where Elizabeth worked, I couldn't help but feel the butterflies in my stomach weren't just from the speed of the elevator.

CHAPTER 5

We walked out into an office that looked like it came straight out of a company's annual report. High ceilings and glass windows went from the floor to ceiling and showed off a million-dollar view of the London skyline—I could see the London Eye, the big famous Ferris wheel, in the distance. Fake potted plants dotted the walls—good fakes, along with modern art that did absolutely nothing for me but that I was sure would have cost more than my entire tuition at Stanford. Men and women in suits scurried efficiently from one side of the office to the other, through a network of glass doors that led to offices and cubicles where I assumed all the business was done. To one side was a receptionist's desk, staffed by a young blonde woman who typed away at a keyboard at a rate that surely couldn't be human while speaking to someone on the phone through her headset.

Violet looked casually around the room, but I knew better now. I knew she saw everything, and I couldn't help but try and copy the way she thought about things. I looked at one of the fake plants and tried to see if there was anything about it that could give me a clue as to the office. I quickly decided no. Perhaps trying on a live subject would be easier. The receptionist. She was left handed! There! That was something, wasn't it?

Before I had a chance to test my skills further, the woman finished her phone call and looked over at us.

"Good morning," she greeted us with a polite smile. She had a high English accent, the same sort as the Queen. She wore a name badge reading "Michaela".

"Hello. Violet Despuis, I called earlier. I'm here to look at the desk of Elizabeth Dalton."

The receptionist's smile immediately fell and was replaced with a look of remorse. "Of course. Poor Lizzie. She was such a nice woman. A bit like a mother to the rest of us girls in reception. Here, let me show you her desk. You'll be wanting to speak with her boss, Leonard Browning, of course. He'll be ready to see you at quarter to ten."

The receptionist led us down a long hallway and into a small office. It was sparsely decorated, with a single framed photo from what looked to be the eighties of a blonde woman standing on a beach with a man. He had his arm around her waist while she laughed, trying to hold her hair back in the wind.

"Her husband," the receptionist told me, noticing my gaze on the photo. "He died in a work accident sometime in the nineties. She never remarried."

"That's too bad," I said. "What was she like, Elizabeth?"

"Oh, Lizzie was a good person. She liked a little bit of gossip, but then, who doesn't? But if you ever had something important, you could always go to Lizzie. When Annie's landlord decided to mess about with her rent last year, it was Lizzie who told her what to do. She was that kind of woman. Very motherly toward us girls. If there was ever any problem, she would help to solve it. She was always asking how we were. Sometimes she'd even bring in cakes from home."

"Has anyone touched Elizabeth's computer since she was killed?" Violet asked, motioning to the desktop sitting in the middle of the desk. The receptionist shook her head.

"No, definitely not. As soon as we found out, Mr. Browning locked her office and told everyone to leave everything as it was until the police got here."

"Good."

I thanked the receptionist, and she smiled at us and left. Looking around the office, I figured Violet would have her work cut out for her. This was the most impersonal space I'd ever seen, really. Apart from the photo, and a small potted plant sitting on the corner of the desk, there barely anything here that said anything about Elizabeth Dalton and the kind of person she was, or who might have wanted her dead.

I ended up mostly standing in the corner, watching as Violet took a portable hard drive from her purse and copied everything from Elizabeth's computer, then she carefully looked around, like she was looking for something.

"Do you notice anything weird?" Violet asked.

I spent about two minutes doing my best to look around and see what Violet was talking about, but eventually I had to admit I was at a loss. "No. There's nothing here *to* see. It's a very plain office."

"*Exactement*. Think of how the receptionist described Elizabeth. Warm. Friendly. She referred to her by a friendly nickname. She brought cakes to the office. By all accounts this place should be covered in horrid knitted cozies and third rate attempts at Pinterest projects. Instead, it is as sterile as an operating theater."

"What does that mean?" I asked Violet, but she shook her head.

"No idea. But it is interesting to note all the same. You never quite know what's going to be important in a case, but you always have to pay attention to it."

About ten minutes later the receptionist came back and led us into the office next door. It was huge; Elizabeth Dalton had obviously been the secretary for one of the firm's head honchos. Decorated as a modern professional's office, it was just as personality-free as Elizabeth's office. The man who got up from the desk to greet us was tall, probably in his early forties if I had to guess. He still had a full head of blond hair, a smile so white that I was sure he got his teeth bleached regularly, and a suit that screamed Italian. I couldn't help but notice that he seemed fairly cheerful for a man whose receptionist had just been brutally murdered, but then, perhaps, that was business.

On his desk was a single personal touch—a posed family portrait. He had his arm around a pretty dark haired woman who must have been his wife, and three young children—two boys and a girl, all completely blonde, stood smiling in front of them.

"Hello," he said, looking at the two of us. I could tell from the extra glance he gave me that he thought I was Violet—the lack of drug inferences on my shirt made it far more likely that I was the one working for the police—but as the receptionist left, Violet held out a hand.

"Violet Despuis, it's nice to meet you," she told the man.

"Leonard Browning. But please, call me Leo. I'm the head of marketing here at Enderby Insurance." He looked over at me questioningly.

"This is my assistant, Cassie." I fought the urge to scowl at Violet. Assistant? I definitely was not. Besides, she invited me here. Instead, I sat in one of the seats Leo motioned us toward and listened as he began to speak.

"An absolute tragedy, of course. Elizabeth was a

great employee. She had been with the firm for two years and I worked quite closely with her. She was efficient, she was diligent, and she will be missed. If there's anything I can do to help find this serial killer, please, I'm more than happy. But I don't know how I can help."

"You think she was killed by a serial killer?" Violet asked, her gaze focused steadily on Leo. He started in surprise.

"Well yes, isn't that the case? It's what all the papers have been saying."

"No, Mr. Browning," Violet said, leaning forward carefully. "Elizabeth was definitely, deliberately murdered."

The man inhaled sharply, then regained his composure.

"I'm so sorry to hear that. But I'm afraid I have no idea who could have done it. I'm afraid that outside of work, I didn't really know Elizabeth that well."

"Who was the one who ordered no one to touch anything in Elizabeth's office?"

"That was me. I locked it as soon as I found out."

"Good," Violet replied with a curt nod.

Leo looked over at me. "I'm sorry, you said she's your assistant, but she's not taking any notes or anything?" he asked, confused.

"She's a really terrible assistant," Violet replied, completely deadpan. I had no idea if she was kidding, or what, but, this was definitely awkward.

"I'm afraid I've just forgotten my pen," I said,

pulling out the little moleskin notebook I always kept in my purse just in case—a habit I started back in undergrad—and giving Leo Browning a bit of an embarrassed look.

He looked at me like I really was the worst assistant ever, then passed me a cheap pen that had the Virgin Money logo on it. It seemed even the heads of marketing departments weren't past stealing pens from their local bank.

Violet asked another question. "Can you think of anyone who might have wanted to murder Elizabeth?"

Leo got the hint and dropped the topic of me. "Oh goodness me, no. It certainly couldn't have been anyone working here. She was an excellent worker, and as far as I know she didn't do much socialising with people from here outside the office. It must have been someone in her personal life, and I'm afraid I know nothing about it at all."

"So you do not know of any disagreements between herself and anyone else in the office?"

"Nothing of the sort, no."

"Did she work on anything that could have been considered sensitive?"

"Of course not. She was only a secretary. She handled most of my correspondence. And to be quite honest, I highly doubt any of our competition would be murdering anybody simply to discover what rates we pay to put our ads on television, or for the design of our latest tube ad."

Violet nodded. "Yes, of course." I scribbled the answers on my little notepad as fast as I could, but honestly, I didn't feel like Leo Browning was giving us any sort of meaningful information. It seemed like he knew very little about his secretary at all.

"Do you know who she might have been close to in the office?" Violet asked, and Browning thought for a minute, then shook his head.

"I'm afraid not. As far as I knew, she really didn't do much socializing at all. She was a very diligent worker."

"All right, thank you for your time," Violet replied, standing up and shaking his hand. I stood up as well and followed Violet as she strode out, feeling a little bit like a little duckling trying to keep up with its mother.

"Your assistant?" I asked when we were back in the hallway, alone.

"I like to practice lying to people. It makes me a better liar. You should do it as well; you are a terrible liar."

"That's not true!" I protested.

"It is. For example, I know you still hate cashew cream."

Damn. She had me there. "Fine. So you practice lying to people for fun?"

"Not for fun. For practice. Everything takes practice. People who tell you they are naturally good liars; they are lying to you. It is not that they are naturally good at it; it is that they lie a lot. So you start small. When the lady at the supermarket asks you if you have plans for the day, you lie and make something up. The stakes are low. What does it matter? She will never know that you are lying, and she almost certainly does not care either. Then as you get more comfortable, you begin lying more often. Not when it matters. Not at first. But the more you practice, the better you get."

I wasn't sure if I should laugh out loud, take Violet's new lesson seriously, or call an insane asylum and tell them I had a new client for them. I was fairly certain the answer was a combination of all three, but before I could tell her that, we arrived back at the lobby of the Enderby Insurance offices, where the receptionist was happily speaking with DCI Williams, who had brought another detective along with him. As soon as he saw Violet, he frowned and came over to see us.

"What are you doing here?" he asked.

"Doing your investigation for you, before the case gets so cold you never find your killer." Violet replied. "If you think it is a serial killer, why are you at one of the victims' workplace?" She smiled smugly, Violet must have known where this was going. DCI Williams ran his hand through his ginger hair, obviously a little bit embarrassed.

"Yes, well, I had a bit of a chat with the Superintendent, and we decided that maybe there is something to this little theory of yours. So I'm here, and I sent a couple of the other guys to check out the other victims' places, to see if we can maybe narrow it down and find out who the target was."

"You might as well call them off. You're the only one doing important work. Elizabeth Dalton was your target."

"You cannot possibly know that."

"I can, and I do. But if you want to continue wasting your time, please do not let me stop you. God knows the men you sent elsewhere will almost certainly not get anything important there."

DCI Williams sighed. "Fine. I'll call them off. Listen, after we're done here we're going to Dalton's home, if you wanted to have a look around. I have a crew there already, and at the other homes. I suppose I should call them off as well."

"Sure. We'll wait here until you're done," Violet said. DCI Williams looked over at me, and gave Violet a curious look, which she ignored. I was beginning to realize that being around Violet meant awkward moments abounded. I wasn't sure if she understood the social convention was to explain why the random girl with the missing bike was hanging around with her, but she just chose to ignore it. Eventually, I broke in.

"Violet invited me here," I explained. "She thought my medical knowledge might come in handy."

"Ah," DCI Williams replied, looking somehow even more confused than before. "Well, there's a first time for everything."

"What did he mean by that?" I asked Violet when he left.

"DCI Williams is under the impression that I am not good with people."

"I wonder how he got that idea," I muttered, almost to myself, then realized Violet heard, and was laughing just a little bit.

"It is true; I am not the greatest at the social skills. But I am so good at other things that it does not matter, he has to put up with me all the same. As I must with him. Now, we go to the Dalton home. We will see what there is for us to discover there."

"Didn't you just tell DCI Williams we would wait here for him?

"He will know where we went. I have changed my mind. We will go now. Remember: when you simply say you have changed your mind, they cannot prove you lied in the first place."

Yeah, there was definitely a little bit of crazy in Violet Despuis.

As we headed back down to the ground floor, I found myself actually interested in what we might manage to find at the Dalton residence.

CHAPTER 6

*E*lizabeth Dalton lived in a small one-bedroom apartment, just a ten-minute walk from where she worked. Violet and I walked to Crawford Street and found her address quite easily, a couple blocks west of Baker Street. She lived in a gorgeous Victorian-era building made of yellowish-orange brick, with wrought-iron balconies in every apartment leaning out over the street. The white framed windows had a gorgeous square pattern along the top, giving the building a super classy look. This place had to be expensive!

"How much would a place like this cost?" I asked Violet.

"Oh, probably around half a million pounds," she replied, and my mouth dropped open.

"Seriously? For a one bedroom?"

"A one bedroom that's just steps away from central London."

"How on earth could someone on a receptionist's salary afford a tiny apartment worth half a million pounds?" I asked. That was like, three quarters of a million dollars!

"I do not know. We will go and find out," Violet said, leading me to the front door. Seeing as there were two marked police cars between a dark unmarked van that screamed *cops* despite obviously trying to do the opposite, it was safe to assume that DCI Williams' crew had in fact arrived first. We entered the building and walked up two flights of stairs, where all the commotion was happening. The door of the apartment that obviously belonged to Elizabeth was being guarded by a uniformed officer, and a nervous-looking fat man with squirrely eyes kept looking around.

"Are you the building manager?" Violet asked the man.

"Excuse me, miss, I'm afraid this is a police matter, you're going to have to leave," the uniformed officer told Violet.

"I'm with the police," Violet replied confidently.

"Oh yes?" the man replied, looking her up and down. He must have been barely twenty. "Where are your credentials, then?"

"*Mon dieu,*" she sighed. "You get on the phone with DCI Williams right now, you tell him Violet Despuis is here, and that she absolutely hates it when police stupidity gets in the way of her doing his job for him in a timely manner."

At the sound of her name, the man's eyes widened.

"Oh, I'm sure there's no need for that, Miss Despuis. My apologies. Please, do as you wish!" The poor kid looked like he was terrified Violet was going to eat him alive, or something.

"Now, where were we? Ah, yes. You are the building manager, are you not?" she asked the fat man again. He looked like he wanted to be anywhere but there, and his eyes darted over to the officer, who nodded, before he answered.

"Yes, madam. I mean, miss. Yes, I'm the manager here. Never had anything like this happen in any of my buildings before, you see? This is a classy part of London. People don't usually get murdered around here."

"Well, relax, it's not like she was murdered in your building."

"Yeah, well, I know that, don't I? But all the same, having all these cops around. I'm not used to that sort of thing, see?"

"I understand. I want you to answer a few questions for me though. Is that all right?"

"Go on then, but I already answered a load for those other coppers."

"I need you to answer some more for me."

"Yeah, all right then, miss."

"First of all, how long had Elizabeth Dalton lived here?"

"Ohh a long time, miss. The property belonged to

her husband, his parents gave it to them as a wedding gift a number of years ago. When he died, I thought she might move. But in the end she stayed. A lonely lady, that one."

"So she isn't the type to get a lot of visitors?"

"Nah. I don't think I've seen anyone come to her flat in at least six months. And even then, I'm fairly certain the visitor was a plumber or some sort."

"Do you know of any friends; anyone she was close to?" Violet asked, but the landlord shook his head sadly.

"No, nothing like that. Quite sad, really. A nice lady like that, she should have had friends. She was always ready to lend a helping hand. Made me chicken soup last year when I had the flu, she did. But she liked to keep to herself. Never really opened up."

"Thank you," Violet told him. "Thank you for your help."

"Excuse me, miss?"

"Yes?" Violet asked, turning back around to the man.

"Please tell me you're going to find the person who did this to her. A woman like that, she didn't deserve that kind of end, you know?"

"Of course I will find them," Violet replied. I stared at her, shocked. *Everyone* knew you weren't supposed to promise anyone results.

"Why did you tell him that?" I asked her in a hushed tone.

"Because it is true," she replied.

"Seriously? You've *never* failed before?" I asked, sceptically. At the same time, I remembered everything she'd told me about myself just the day before, and I started to think that maybe she wasn't going to tell me that yes, she had failed.

"I have failed," she replied. "But it has been rare. Four times. Three killers, and one robber are free. And of the killers, I know who one of them is; I simply was never able to bring them to justice. The same with the robber."

"How many cases have you done?" I asked, curiosity getting the better of me.

"Several hundred. At least."

I let out a low whistle. Ok, she had a reason to be pretty confident. We walked past the officer guarding the door, who looked like he was trying to melt into the wall as Violet walked past him, and made our way into the little one-bedroom place.

A half dozen police officers were scouring the place, searching, evidently, for anything that might lead to a motive for Elizabeth Dalton's death. The apartment was entirely visible from the entrance where we were standing, and it was exactly what I'd expected. It was cozy, with old-style upholstery on the small couch. Chintzy little figurines adorned the mantelpiece above the gas fireplace, and a police officer rummaged through a bag of knitting needles and yarn sitting next to the couch.

But for all her old-style decorating, Elizabeth Dalton was evidently a little bit of a big spender as well. A new iPad sat on the little side table on the other side of the couch, on a stand in front of it was a giant TV, at least fifty inches, with one of those slightly curved screens to give off that theater effect. A brand new KitchenAid sat on the counter in the small kitchen, and I spotted what I was fairly certain was a Prada handbag poking out from the bedroom.

Before I got a chance to go in and have a look, however, I felt something at my feet. I looked down to find a little orange cat meowing at me. He raised a paw and tapped me on the leg, then meowed again. I looked around, but none of the police officers seemed to even notice him. I wondered if the poor thing had been here alone for two days now.

"Ummm, I don't know if anyone has fed the cat," I told Violet, motioning down at him.

"Awww, he's a little cutie, isn't he?" she said. She raised her voice. "Has anyone done anything to deal with the cat at all since Dalton's death?"

A murmur of negatives came flooding back from the cops.

"You're all a bunch of morons," she suddenly added. "Just because you have one dead body to take care of doesn't mean you can just leave the cat here to become a second victim."

"We don't have time to deal with a cat," one of the officers complained. "We have a murder to solve."

"Yes, Watkins, I'm sure you're hot on the trail and definitely seconds away from finding the murderer as you continue to investigate the dirt on the floor that's obviously come from your own shoes."

Watkins looked down and his face flushed red with embarrassment. I had to stifle a laugh, and instead picked up the cat, who happily leapt up onto my shoulder as I made my way into the kitchen. I took out a tissue and carefully opened the cabinet doors—I wasn't sure what I was and wasn't allowed to touch—and took out a plate and a can of cat food. The little cat jumped onto the counter and paced around the plate while I found a can opener, and as soon as I'd placed a little bit on the plate for him, he dug in like he hadn't eaten in days, poor thing.

I had never really been a cat person. I'd never been a pet person. We didn't have the money to own one growing up, and obviously when I was in college, on top of having no money, that wasn't exactly the right time to take on that kind of responsibility. Still, I felt a little tinge of guilt when the cat finished all his food and looked up at me, wanting more.

"Sorry buddy, I don't know anything about cats, but if you haven't eaten in days it's probably not a good idea to eat too much all at once," I told him, daring to move over and rub his head. "Elizabeth didn't mean to leave you here for a couple days without any food, little guy. I promise you that."

Violet was now looking around the apartment, walking from room to room, looking carefully at everything Elizabeth Dalton had owned. I filled up a bowl with water and left it for the cat, who began drinking happily, then followed her into the bedroom. Sure enough, it was a Prada purse on the ground. When Violet opened the closet, there was a Marc Jacobs and a Louis Vuitton there as well.

"Those are real, right?" I asked Violet. Having grown up in the Bay Area, I was pretty good at being able to tell a real designer bag from a fake. Both abounded all over San Francisco.

"They certainly are," she replied thoughtfully, fingering the clothes in the closet. I moved into the bathroom and had a look in the medicine cabinet. I checked the labels on the few bottles that were there: low dose oestrogen pills and bisphospho-nates. Elizabeth Dalton had apparently hit menopause, and was likely beginning to suffer from osteoporosis. I said this to Violet, who had moved to the entrance of the bathroom and was looking around carefully.

"Interesting," she said.

"Does it mean anything?" I asked, but she shrugged.

"I do not know. I have an idea, right now. It is just that though, an idea. Not fully formed. We will discuss it later. So far, the medicines there do not fall in with my idea, but they do not have to. It is still too early to know for sure what is important and what is not."

We were suddenly interrupted by the little orange cat who had found me once again and sat down on my feet, looking up at me and meowing.

"It seems he has found the person most likely to feed him, and is becoming attached," Violet told me.

"How do you know it's a him?"

"Nearly all orange cats are male. It is a genetic thing. For a female cat to be orange, she must inherit the orange gene from both parents, meaning that her mother must be orange, calico or tortoiseshell in color, *and* her father must be orange as well. For a male cat, however, the orange gene needs only to be inherited from the mother, as the color gene is on the X chromosome. Any male cat born to a mother who is orange, calico or tortoiseshell in color will be orange. Therefore, approximately eighty percent of orange cats are male."

"Huh. I didn't know that. Well, little guy, maybe I can give you another tablespoon or so of food, if you promise not to puke it up everywhere."

"Also, if you lift his tail you will notice his sex organ is rounded, not a vertical slit like it would be in a female cat," Violet continued. I was learning more than I'd ever thought I'd know about cats today.

I made my way back to the kitchen, the little orange ball of fluff following right on my tail.

Placing another spoonful of food on the plate, he happily ate it all up, his tail moving slowly from side to side as he did. When he was finished, he looked up at me expectantly.

"Not yet, little guy," I told him. "I need to find out what your name is."

I had a quick look around the apartment, trying

not to get in the way of the police officers who I couldn't help but notice looked at me as a bother, but didn't dare say anything in front of Violet. When I started looking at Elizabeth Dalton's iPad, I opened up her Facebook account and found an album in her photos labeled *Biscuit*. A cursory glance confirmed that the little ball of fur begging for more food was the aptly named Biscuit.

"All right, Biscuit, you have to wait at least ten more minutes before I'm giving you anymore," I told him, and he meowed at me loudly, as if in protest. Violet laughed as she came over and took the iPad.

"Do you mind if I have a look?" she asked, and I handed it over. After all, I reminded myself, this was a murder investigation. I may have solved the mystery of the cat's name, but he had belonged to a woman who'd been killed, and we still had no idea who was responsible.

Fifteen minutes later, Violet announced that we were finished here.

"What about the cat?" I asked. She motioned to the cops, all of whom were moving around the apartment, absorbed in their work.

"They are not going to do anything for him. Pack of heartless morons, all of them."

"I'll report to DCI Williams that you said that," one of them called out.

"Then I'll report to him that you're sleeping with DI Marshall," Violet called out in reply. One of the women looking behind the television let out a small squeal, and the complaining about Violet's insults stopped. I had to hand it to her; she knew how to both annoy people, and how to get what she wanted. "I suggest you take Biscuit back with you," she offered.

"But how?" I asked, eyeing an empty shoebox and wondering just how much the cat would claw me if I walked him back to the hostel in that.

"There's a leash with a harness attached behind the coats on the rack," Violet said, motioning with her head toward the entrance. Great. When I'd planned this trip I'd envisioned myself confidently strolling through the streets of London, a cosmopolitan young traveler getting over her depression and conquering the world with her head held high, not wandering through the streets with a cat on a leash like a crazy person. Still, it beat the shoebox. As soon as I grabbed the leash Biscuit came running up, and thankfully calmly allowed me to put the leash on. At least all the scarring I was going to get from this experience would be mental, not physical.

"All right, Biscuit, let's go," I told him. Biscuit was obviously used to walking on the leash and led the way as the three of us made our way back outside. Violet guided us toward Bryanston Square, a couple blocks from the apartment, where we sat while Biscuit eyed the pigeons hungrily. I doubled up my grip on his leash, just to be safe.

"So what did you think?" Violet asked when we sat down on a bench in the square. It was nice; large trees and hedges blocked the view of the city around us, although they couldn't dim the sound of traffic from the major roads nearby—Baker Street on one side and Edgware Road on the other. A nice breeze rustled the leaves on the trees, as Biscuit did his best to kill the leaves drifting slowly to the ground. I liked these quiet little nooks of London. They were peaceful, they were nice. Little pods of peace in the middle of the busy city.

"I'm not sure," I said slowly. "I mean, the apartment was more along the lines of what I expected from someone like Elizabeth, given what the receptionist told us. All those little cat figurines on the mantelpiece, the knitting, that sort of thing. And yet, at the same time, something didn't really seem right about it."

"*C'est ça,*" Violet replied, nodding. "And I will tell you what was not right, it was the expensive toys."

"Yeah, they seemed a bit weird. I mean, everyone's grandma's place looks like Elizabeth's, but most people's grandmas hate technology."

"It is not just the technology. It is the handbags. It is the expensive kitchen appliances. Most people's grandmothers are frugal, they do not wish to spend any money. And that is partly evidenced in Mrs. Dalton's flat. She still has the old sofa, the old furniture. And yet, also the new shiny toys. And they are new. None of those toys are older than six months."

"Really? How do you know?"

"The Prada bag is from the spring catalogue, the

Marc Jacobs and the Louis Vuitton were released only a couple of weeks ago. The KitchenAid has been used maybe three times. We have heard what kind of woman Elizabeth Dalton was; she would have baked cakes and used it regularly. No, she did not buy that more than one month ago. There was a receipt for the iPad and the TV in the wastepaper basket."

"So lately she's been spending all her money, on fancy things."

"Yes, and that in and of itself is quite telling, no? It implies that either a situation changed and made her more willing to spend money in the last few months, or that she has come into a new source of money in that time. After all, a receptionist, even for so powerful a man as Leonard Browning, would not be making more than thirty thousand pounds per year."

"So you think she's a drug dealer or something? That seems unlikely."

"Never assume!" Violet exclaimed in reply. "Never, ever assume! I once caught an eighty-four-year-old lady who had robbed eight jewellery stores of diamonds worth over fifteen million pounds in total. Another time, a man in a wheelchair killed six people he didn't like. I also once caught a secondary school student running a million-pound drug empire from his school's computer lab. You can never assume anything about anyone. Only follow the facts."

"All right, all right," I said, throwing up my hands. Another small breeze blew past and Biscuit began trying to pounce on the moving leaves at our feet. "So what happens now? We have to figure out why she suddenly decided she was going to spend money?"

"Exactly! Had she found out she was dying? Did she have only a couple of months to live and want to enjoy the rest of her time on earth? Most people, if that is the case, they go traveling and not shopping."

I shook my head. "No, definitely not. She had menopause, and I suspect given the low dose estrogen she was given there was a small chance of depression associated with it, but those were the only drugs I found in her apartment. If she had cancer or something there would have likely been much more evidence of it."

"You are almost certainly correct. All the same, I believe we should go speak with the coroner. He should have the autopsy done by tomorrow morning. Would you like to come?"

"I would, yes," I replied. I was interested now; I was invested in this case. I needed to know what was going to happen.

"Good. I would like you there, just in case. He is not as dumb as the police, the medical examiner. He is in fact quite intelligent. But I find that those who deal exclusively with the dead have a tendency to forget that those people were once living, and as such sometimes their judgement is clouded. I will call you."

"Yes, please call! I think I'll have a heart attack if I

wake up finding you sitting on my bed again," I replied as Violet got up.

"It was important that you came with me. You are good for the thoughts. It turns out that speaking everything aloud to someone who responds is a good way to stimulate the thought process. Good afternoon, Cassie. I will see you tomorrow."

I was half expecting Violet to drop a smoke bomb and disappear, but instead she simply casually strolled down to the edge of the square and back onto the street, staring at the ground, obviously deep in thought. Biscuit looked after her, then looked after me.

"Ready to go little guy? Let's see if we can't sneak you into the hostel. I really need to find a new place to live."

CHAPTER 7

I was extremely thankful that the hostel was only a bit over ten minutes away from the square. I felt like everyone was staring at me for walking through the street with a cat on a leash. Biscuit, to his credit, was incredibly good about it, and not self-conscious at all. He happily strode up the street, letting himself be pet, meowing at strangers, and generally being adorable, while I did my best to shrink into the scenery. At least no one looked at me like I was a crazy person. Not to my face, at least.

Luckily, sneaking Biscuit into the hostel was a lot easier than the bike. I just shoved the little guy into my purse for thirty seconds while I walked into the building, and made my way into my room. As an added bonus, it seemed my German roommate was gone; the bed next to mine was now devoid of occupants. Ah well, this was a hostel in central London. It wouldn't be long before I had a new roomie for a few days.

And that was a problem. I let Biscuit out of my purse and let him wander around the room, where he sniffed the corners for a minute before happily settling on top of my pillow. Check-in wasn't for another three hours, I probably had time to go out and get some cat supplies and a bit of lunch, I thought to myself. Promising Biscuit I'd be back, I searched Google, trying to find a pet store near me. Unfortunately, the pickings were slim. I ended up heading to the local grocery store, where I thankfully found a small supply of cat food, and a single litter box with litter included. Thank goodness. I'd hopefully be able to find a better place elsewhere later, but this would have to do for now.

I went back to the hostel and set up the litter box at the foot of my bed for Biscuit then headed out to grab lunch. I'd promised myself after breakfast with Violet that lunch would be a greasy slice of pizza, but when I found out there was a Chipotle on Baker Street, I was sold! I made my way back over there, avoiding Crawford Street lest I saw one of the police officers from this morning, and found my favorite Mexican restaurant. There was no line when I went in, and three minutes later the cashier was ringing up my order. She was a little bit on the short side, but with a pretty face framed by short red hair.

"Any plans for today?" she asked, with a strong Australian accent. I immediately thought back to what Violet said about practicing lying. And what she said about how bad I was at lying. There was no way that was a real thing, right? It was ridiculous to even *consider* trying it. After all, who does that? Nobody. It was just Violet being Violet. Violet being the weirdest person I knew. There was no way I could do it. There was no way I *would* do it. After all, wasn't that the sort of thing a psycho would do? Practice lying to people who wouldn't know the difference?

And yet, my mouth opened and a lie came out. "Oh, not much, just grabbing some lunch before starting a shift at work."

What the hell? What was I doing? I was lying to a complete stranger. Why? Why would I do that? Because the world's weirdest person told me I should try it? That was so not a good enough reason. My face flamed red, I could tell. I could just tell it was on fire. Great. The girl knew I was lying. She had to know. Oh God, Violet had been right about how bad I was at lying. I was about to get caught, and it would be so awkward.

"Cool, where do you work?" she asked as I handed over a ten pound note, trying to keep my hands from trembling.

"Oh… ummmm…" I started. I hadn't expected any follow-up questions, or for her to even believe my lie. "McDonalds," I replied, the first thing that came into my head.

"Nice. Working retail sucks, hey? Have a good one."

"Thanks, you too," I replied, grabbing my burrito and practically running out of the store. My face was on fire with embarrassment. She knew. Surely she had known that I'd been lying to her.

Oh God, I was so embarrassed. Why had I done that? I'd just made a total idiot of myself, and now I was never, ever going to be able to go back to Chipotle again. At least, not when that girl was working, anyway. My face burned as I made my way back to the hostel. That was the most embarrassing thing I'd ever done. I had no idea why I'd done it, either. It was crazy! Who lies to people, just to practice? Ugh.

I was still completely mortified, and ashamed of myself, when I got back into my room. Biscuit was very happy to see me, and tried more than once to steal part of my burrito. I had to laugh at his covert attempts at being subtle, which basically involved trying to smack the burrito at top speed with the goal of making the filling fall out.

Eventually I gave in and gave him a couple chunks of chicken, which he happily lapped up. He was a real cutie, and I thought to myself that I really, seriously had to get myself my own place. After all, I couldn't secretly keep a cat in the hostel forever, and if I got caught I'd get kicked out of here for sure.

I laid down to rest my head for a little bit, and the next thing I knew I'd had a ninety-minute nap. I woke up to find Biscuit contentedly sleeping away in the crook of my neck. As it turned out, finding a murderer was really hard work. But at least one good thing had come from it, I thought as I reached up to pet Biscuit softly.

Luckily for me, that night I didn't have a new roommate to try and explain my new cat to. Once again, I browsed rental sites looking for something in my price range. Finally, I made the decision to increase my budget a little, so I could find something liveable sooner rather than later. I also had never realized until acquiring Biscuit just how many rental places had a no pets rule.

I sent off a dozen emails to potential places, hoping to be able to get a viewing soon, then went out and grabbed a quick dinner before going back to sleep, wondering what kind of crazy tomorrow was going to bring.

CHAPTER 8

$\mathcal{T}$he next day my phone buzzed just after eight in the morning.

Ready at the medical examiners. Meet you outside in ten minutes.

Ten minutes? Jeez, how quickly did Violet think I could get ready? Luckily I'd gone to bed so early the night before that I was already awake and showered, so I brushed my hair quickly, tied it back into a quick ponytail and threw on a pair of leggings and a long-sleeved black shirt. It was more casual than business, but I didn't think the medical examiner would care too much how I was dressed.

I quickly put some cat food into a bowl, prayed that no one from the hostel would come into the room until I came back, and left while Biscuit was still happily eating, or more accurately, inhaling his food.

Violet was waiting for me outside the hostel in

skinny jeans and a Run DMC t-shirt, with a messenger bag slung over her shoulder.

"Good," she said in greeting when I came out. "We will be at the coroner's office to meet with the pathologist in fifteen minutes," she said, hailing a cab on the street.

"Do the cops pay your expenses?" I asked. After all, I knew a cab downtown was around fifteen pounds, whereas taking the underground would only be a couple pounds.

"No," Violet replied. "They do not pay me anything. I just pick and choose the cases I want to work."

"How do you make your money then, if you don't mind me asking?"

"You Americans," she replied. "It is funny to be around you. You have no qualms about asking about anything. No English person would ever ask me that."

"Sorry," I said, feeling chastised.

"*Non, non.* You misunderstand me. I did not say it was a bad thing. I simply say it as a fact. Most of my work is not in fact with the police. Often I take private cases. And I am a socialist at heart. The bigger the client, the more they must pay. I take from the rich, and I give the money to me. I am half Robin Hood."

I laughed. "So you weren't born into money then."

"Oh, I was. But I have not spoken with my family in a very long time. I assume I am completely disowned. I make my own money. And I make a lot of it."

"Did you come up with any other ideas last night as to why Elizabeth Dalton was killed?"

"I have four promising theories. None of them involve her spending money because she was dying, so I will be quite disappointed if Doctor Edmonds tells us that she had terminal cancer."

"Ah, so even the great Violet Despuis can have opinions, instead of simply waiting on the facts," I teased.

"I do have opinions, yes. But also, conclusions! Conclusions that I never come to without having the facts. I do not deny that sometimes I hope that the facts will support the conclusions that I have determined to be the most likely."

Fifteen minutes later we were standing in front of an old red brick building with an imposing air about it. It was surrounded by a red brick wall and red iron gate, and looked exactly what I'd imagined an English government building would look like—though it was a bit smaller than I'd expected. Gold lettering adorned a dark red sign that matched the hue of the iron gate and read "Coroner's Court". This was quite possibly the most British corner in all of London. Next to the building was a red telephone box—which a double decker bus just happened to be driving past —and directly across the street from the Westminster Coroner's Court was a pub called The Barley Mow, which advertised British food and had a picture of a farm boy sitting in a field of barley hanging above the door. Violet paid the cab fare and the two of us entered the building.

Violet obviously knew where she was going; she led us to an elevator that would take us to the basement level—we were going to the morgue.

The elevator doors opened directly into the morgue. Metallic cubbies holding individual bodies lined the far wall, while five sterile metal tables were aligned directly in front of us. Harsh fluorescent lighting made the white walls and grey tiled floor seem even more clinical. To the left were a few offices, where files on the deceased were obviously kept. Four of the five tables were empty; the fifth held Elizabeth Dalton's body, covered below the neck by a thin white sheet.

"Ah, Miss Despuis, you've arrived, just give me a moment," I heard a voice call out from one of the offices, and a minute later out came the most gorgeous man I'd ever seen in my life.

He looked like he'd just come off a beach in Australia rather than the office of a morgue in London. Over six feet tall with broad shoulders, the man had tousled sandy-blond hair, blue eyes that twinkled in the light and a smile that was definitely making my panties melt. He even had dimples when he smiled. Dimples!

He saw me and held out a hand. I took it, forcing myself to try and act normal instead of allowing myself to completely fawn over him.

"Hi, I'm Doctor Edmonds. Call me Jake, though."

Jake. What a perfect name for this perfect man.

"I'm Cassie," I replied breathlessly, completely failing to keep my voice steady. He shot me a smile and I felt my legs turn to jelly. *Get it together, woman!* I was suddenly reminded of *just* how long it had been since I'd had a boyfriend.

"It's nice to meet you, Cassie," he replied. "You seem like way too nice a girl to be hanging around Violet," he continued with a wink, and I giggled into my hands like a schoolgirl.

"If the two of you would like to have sex right now, I can come back later," Violet said suddenly, and my blood instantly ran cold.

"What?" I practically shrieked at her. I could feel my face flushing with embarrassment. Violet shrugged.

"It is obvious the two of you are attracted to each other. I can leave and come back if you'd like to be alone."

"Oh my God! No!" I cried out. My voice sounded shrill, even to me. "Why would you even ask that?"

"I thought I was being considerate," Violet said, looking a bit confused.

"Ok, well, for the record, offering to leave so I can have sex with a stranger I've just met is *so* not considerate."

I dared a look over at Jake, who was standing there with an amused grin on his face. A gorgeous, adorable amused grin. My face flushed an even deeper shade of red.

"I see you don't know Violet very well," he said. "That's like, number four on the list of embarrassing things she's said to me. Don't worry about it, you get used to her eventually."

"What were the other three?" I asked shrilly, completely incredulous. I was so completely mortified. This made running away from the lady at Chipotle yesterday seem like a walk in the park. The worst part was, Violet was *right*. I would have stripped for a man like that in a minute, but that didn't mean she had to spell it out for him. Oh God. Now I'd never have a chance with him.

"Trust me, you don't want to know. Now, let's see the body."

I'd have liked to have seen his body, I thought to myself, but instead I kept my mouth shut and made sure to stand behind Violet while we went over to Elizabeth Dalton's remains. I still could not believe Violet said that. Seriously!

"I performed the full autopsy yesterday. It will still take time before the official toxicology report is back, but unofficially, as you know, she died of strychnine poisoning."

"Yes, what we're more interested in though is if there were any other long-term health problems she might have had."

"I saw some signs of osteoporosis," Jake replied.

"That's code for he accidentally snapped a bone in

half," I joked to Violet. That was an old medical school joke. Jake laughed.

"Well, you're not wrong. Luckily it was just one of her phalanges, nothing major."

"We found medication in her medicine cabinet, it seems Elizabeth Dalton got punched in the gut pretty badly by menopause. I think she was also slightly depressed."

"That explains that then. I figured it was most likely, but had nothing to confirm. Other than that, however, she seemed to be in perfect health. There was nothing that might indicate she was terminally ill."

"Are you sure?" Violet asked. "No cancers hiding around anywhere? Was the heart muscle slightly thicker than usual?"

"You think it might have been an arrhythmia?" I asked Violet, and I saw Jake look at me, impressed.

"I don't *think* it might have been anything, I'm asking Jake if he checked the size of the heart muscle tissue."

"Believe it or not, Miss Despuis, you're not the only person who's good at their job. I checked the size of the heart tissue, which was normal, and I looked at the tissue slides under the microscope. Completely normal."

"Can I ask something?" I asked, unable to look Jake in the eye. I knew my face still probably looked like a tomato. But could you really blame me? I'd just met the hottest guy ever and the girl next to me had turned it into what was hands down *the* most awkward moment of my life. Violet was a terrible wingman.

"Sure," Jake said, sounding a bit surprised, but open to it. Violet looked at me as well, her gaze penetrating, but solid. She wanted to know what I was going to ask about.

"Did you see any signs of endocarditis?"

"No, the heart valves looked completely normal," Jake replied, and then suddenly a sly smile came onto his face. "Hold on! You brought your own bloody doctor here, you crazy woman," he told Violet. "You don't trust me, so you brought Cassie along."

Violet shrugged. "She's new to London. I'm showing her around the city."

"Your sightseeing tour isn't exactly what most people look for on Trip Advisor."

"Maybe not, but it is certainly more interesting than standing in line at Buckingham Palace."

"Anyway, you're diverting from my point. You've literally brought a doctor here to double check my information. Why did you even bother, you normally do it yourself?"

"I am not a trained doctor, she's likely better at it than I am."

"I'm a trained doctor, and I am a lot better at this than you are."

Violet made a sound in her throat that sounded suspiciously like she disagreed with that second part of the sentence. Jake burst out laughing.

"You're unbelievable. I never thought I'd see you with anyone else. Quite frankly, I didn't think there'd be a lot of people out there willing to take you on."

"This is only my second day with her," I added, which was probably rather unhelpful.

"Well, two days is longer than most people could work with Miss Despuis, so congratulations are in order there Cassie."

I laughed. "She's not that bad once you get to know her."

"No, she's not, is she?" To her credit, Violet was taking the ribbing we were giving her quite well. She had that small smile on her face that I was fairly sure either meant she was amused, or plotting to murder someone. I was sincerely hoping for the former. Either way, she deserved all the ribbing I could give her after that comment. Oh God, that comment. I was never going to get over it.

"If you are both finished making fun of me, I think we're finished here. Doctor Edmonds, always a pleasure."

"You too, Miss Despuis," he replied, shaking her hand, then mine. I actually dared to meet Jake's eyes as he shook my hand, and he winked at me. My face instantly went scarlet, and I babbled a terrible goodbye before practically launching myself back to the elevator.

When we were back outside, I immediately launched on Violet.

"What on *earth* made you say that? That was so embarrassing!"

She simply shrugged. "What? It was obvious the two of you were attracted to each other. I thought I would save you both some time."

"That wasn't saving time! That was making the situation infinitely more awkward!"

"Well, I am sorry, next time I promise not to try to be your—how do you say—wingman."

I couldn't help myself. I burst out laughing at hearing her say that.

"You are the craziest person I have ever met," I replied. I was torn between wanting to punch her and wanting to hug her. I was starting to get the feeling that was how most people thought of Violet.

"While I know you are exaggerating, I would imagine that doing the rounds as a resident you have come across people with mental illnesses with far more destructive symptoms than my own. Now, since you have not yet had breakfast, we will go to a nice place I know not far from here and discuss the findings."

Ugh. The last thing I wanted do was to eat breakfast at another everything-free healthy food place. "Oh, I already ate breakfast," I told Violet, trying to sound casual. I really hoped my lying practice yesterday paid off. She laughed.

"Nice try, but you are still not a good liar. Besides, even if you were, it is obvious you are not telling me the truth."

"Why's that?" I asked. "How could you *possibly* know that?"

"Your hair is slightly wet where your ponytail comes together, which means you showered just before coming out to meet me. And yet, you were still tired enough that you put your shirt on inside out, so you must not have been awake for longer than ten minutes when you got dressed. Not nearly enough time to both shower and have breakfast."

"Damn it," I muttered to myself as I noticed she was right about the shirt. Great. At least the dark fabric didn't make it super obvious, hopefully Doctor Gorgeous down there hadn't noticed that I apparently wasn't able to dress myself like an adult.

"So come on. It is all right, this place has options that will suit your apparent desire to die of a cardiac event prematurely," she continued. I felt a little bit insulted, but also relieved that I wasn't going to have to eat vegetables for breakfast two days in a row, so I followed. It seemed like Violet knew where everything was in this huge city.

"This doesn't mean I've forgiven you yet," I muttered to Violet as we walked off.

CHAPTER 9

*T*wo minutes later we were sitting at a café that made their coffee with real milk—actually spelled with an "i"—and I sipped a very normal tasting latte contentedly while perusing the menu. Violet was doing the same thing while sitting across from me with a green smoothie. As far as I was concerned, spinach and kale were not foods that belonged in smoothies. I had just settled on the French toast topped with berries and maple syrup when Violet put down her menu with a thud.

"I'm now down to two theories," Violet said suddenly. "Possibly three."

"She's not a drug dealer, and she didn't just spend all her money because she was dying of cancer?" I asked.

"*Exactement*," Violet replied. "It was good that you asked about the endocarditis."

I knew from medical school that there were two

major ways to tell if someone had been addicted to drugs when doing an autopsy. Of course there were the usual outward signs: track marks, and that sort of thing. But not all drugs were shot up, and not all drugs had outward signs of use, especially if the person taking them only did so recreationally, which I imagined Elizabeth Dalton would have, had she partaken. The first was a thickening in the heart walls, as Violet had asked about. The second was checking for endocarditis in the heart valve. Basically, bacteria gets stuck on the heart valve and shows up as red-tan growths in an autopsy. If she'd had them, it would have meant that Elizabeth Dalton had almost certainly used intravenous drugs, though perhaps not often enough for track marks to be obvious.

"So what are the two options left?" I asked.

"Blackmail and embezzlement. They are the most likely, at any rate. I still haven't ruled out an inheritance from a long-lost relative, but it seems unlikely. I have a man checking probate records for me now."

"Which one do you think it is?"

"Have you learned nothing yet? It could be either! I do not know, and I do not speculate. But after breakfast, we go back to the offices of Elizabeth Dalton, and we ask if we can look at their financial records."

The waiter came over and took our orders—I didn't even know what the Buddha bowl Violet ordered *was*—and Violet leaned forward.

"So how is the flat search coming along?"

I shrugged. "I've upped my budget, and I've emailed a few places, but I can't really find anything. It's tough, because I know as soon as Biscuit gets discovered in my room I'm going to get kicked out. I just hope I manage to find something before it gets to that point."

Violet smiled at me. "Well luckily for you, I have found you an apartment."

"Really?" I asked, surprised.

"Yes. It turns out that one of my neighbors, Mrs. Michaels, who has been a widow for a number of years, is currently searching for a new tenant for the one-bedroom flat below her home, as the previous one has moved in with her boyfriend. If you would like, I can make the introduction."

"Wow, thank you! That would be great!" I exclaimed. "I have to admit though, I am surprised. You don't seem to be the type to, well, socialize with your neighbors all that much."

Violet smiled slyly. "Perhaps not. But a little while back I helped Mrs. Michaels with a spot of trouble she was having with the police. She has been quite partial to me ever since."

"Ah." That made a lot more sense. Somehow, I just couldn't picture Violet Despuis going over to her neighbors' for afternoon tea and book club every few weeks.

"*Parfait*. She is ready for you to move in whenever."

"So when you said you'd make an introduction…" I said, letting the sentence hang, and Violet finished it for me.

"I meant that I had already agreed that you would take the suite. Below market rate, of course. Do not worry, it is perfectly fine. It is a one-bedroom, the kitchen and bathroom were fully renovated a few years ago, and Mrs. Michaels is a very quiet woman who will not bother you much at all. There is even a small garden at the back that you have full access to, as Mrs. Michaels is afraid of spiders and refuses to go near any of the plants on the off chance one might be living there."

"Oh, Violet, you're too kind. You didn't have to do that!" I exclaimed.

"But it is in my best interest as well. I like speaking out my theories to you, and if you are ever going to be coming along with me in the future, I would rather you live down the street than in Essex."

I smiled to myself. Only Violet could take a favor and turn it into a reason as to how it made things easier for her.

"Either way, thank you. I really appreciate it."

Violet waved away my thanks just as the waiter reappeared with a heaping plate of pancakes that I noticed Violet actually made a half-effort to not scowl at.

Half an hour later we were fed and sitting in a taxi once more, heading back to Enderby Insurance.

"So what do we do? Go up there and ask if anyone

knew Elizabeth Dalton was embezzling?" I asked.

"That is a blunt, and normally a rather ineffective method. No, we are not going to do that. We will ask to see the financial records of the company. After all, Mr. Browning told us he was willing to do anything to help find her murderer. We will see just how much he meant those words."

When we got to the Enderby Insurance offices, however, the receptionist told us Mr. Browning was unavailable. We were, however, able to speak with his second-in-command if we wanted, and Violet indicated that yes, we did want.

We sat on a long, modern-style couch behind the reception area in a lobby decorated with modern, if inoffensive art—the type of art that would never offend anyone, but screamed expensive all the same. About five minutes later a tall woman in her mid-thirties with short black hair in a pixie cut came out. She was efficient, and all business.

"Are you the two here with the police?" she asked us, and we stood up. Violet held out a hand.

"Violet Despuis."

"Oh! *The* Violet Despuis? It's very nice to meet you," the woman said. "I'm Jennifer Ashton, the marketing strategies manager here at Enderby. Please, follow me to my office." We got up and followed her as Jennifer continued talking. "Unfortunately Leo was called away on business, he's in Paris for a couple of days, but he should be back tomorrow afternoon. It's such a tragedy about what happened to Elizabeth. She seemed like quite a nice woman. She had great taste in fashion as well. Of course, I didn't really know her *well*, only really to say hello and ask if Mr. Browning was available, but the short time we did chat, I liked her. I can't believe anyone would want to kill someone like that. What can I help you with?" she asked as she led us into an office which was noticeably smaller than Leonard Browning's, but otherwise looked identical, designed in that super modern style.

"We were hoping to be able to have a look at the finances of the company," Violet said. "We suspect there's a possibility that Elizabeth Dalton was embezzling money, and that perhaps her murderer may have realized it."

The smile completely fell off Jennifer's face. "My goodness! You think she was killed on purpose! I thought it was an accident."

"It most certainly was not," Violet replied. "I know it is a lot to ask. However, I promise you, my discretion, and that of Miss Coburn's here, is impeccable. Mr. Browning promised us when we spoke to him the last time that he would do whatever was necessary to help in the investigation into Miss Dalton's death."

Jennifer pursed her lips slightly. I could tell she was trying to decide what to do.

"All right, I have to be honest here. I can't take your word for it that Mr. Browning said it would be all right, and while I want to help you, I also want to keep my job. You're working with the police, but you don't have a warrant or anything, so I can't simply give you access to all of the financial information of the company. What I can do, however, is convene a meeting with the top executives of the company. Then when they've decided what to do, I can give you a call. How does that sound?"

The tone of her voice made it evident that there were going to be no other offers.

"That would be fine, thank you," Violet told her, pulling a business card from her wallet and handing it to Jennifer. "I would please ask that you come to your decision quickly, as there is a murderer out there somewhere in London, and very possibly within the walls of your organization," she added, her eyes boring into Jennifer's, whose eyes widened slightly at the mention.

"You don't think it could be someone who works here," she said almost breathlessly. "Surely not."

"Just because you do hundreds of millions of pounds per year in business doesn't mean there isn't a murderer somewhere in this building," Violet replied, standing up.

"I promise you, Miss Despuis, I will ensure you have a reply by close of business. And I will do my best to ensure the board makes the right decision and grants you access to the records you seek."

"Thank you, Ms. Ashton," Violet replied. Evidently she'd scared the poor woman into going straight to the board for permission.

We both shook Jennifer Ashton's hand once more, promising her that we could find our own way back to reception, and made our way back into the hallway of offices. Instead of going straight to reception, however, Violet headed in the opposite direction.

"What are you doing?" I hissed.

"Just taking a quick detour. Don't worry about it. Walk like you know where you're going, no one will stop us."

I tried to do as Violet asked, making a point of not looking in any of the offices we passed. When we hit the end of the hallway, there was a stairwell leading back down to the ground floor; we were so high up I imagined it was only ever used as an emergency exit. Violet took her phone out and snapped a quick picture of the map on the wall with the company's evacuation plan. I didn't even want to know why she needed that; there was no way she could possibly need that for anything legal.

"Good, they were cheap and put all three floors on a single map," she said, looking at it. Then, slipping her phone back into her purse, Violet led us back toward the reception area.

She smiled at Michaela before we left. "I was wondering," she said. "Would you happen to have any pictures of Elizabeth, from work? You know, just candid shots? Anything like that? Recent would be best."

"Oh, sure!" the receptionist replied cheerily. "We

had a retirement party for Albert Donaghey a few weeks ago, then of course the Christmas party a few months back. I have a couple of other photos as well. They generally put me in charge of that sort of thing, there's a lady in HR who does up a staff newsletter every month, and she likes to have pictures for it. I'll email them to you."

"That would be great," Violet replied, handing her a business card. "Thank you. And if you wouldn't mind, could you send some of the older issues of the newsletters as well?"

"Of course! Listen, is it true what people are saying?" The receptionist dropped her voice. "That Lizzie was killed on purpose? Like, she was targeted instead of it being random?"

"That is correct. Someone killed her on purpose."

The receptionist gave a furtive glance around. "Can you meet me outside in fifteen minutes? I don't want to say anything here. Out the back entrance."

"Of course," Violet said, and turned and left without another word.

"Why did you ask for those?" I asked Violet when we left.

"I am trying to get as much information as possible about Elizabeth Dalton. It seems increasingly likely that whatever happened to her was related to her work somehow, and I like to have as much information as possible that's not been tainted by people's insane inability to make the slightest negative comment concerning the dead."

"So you think she was embezzling."

"I did not say that. We have no proof she was embezzling."

"Right, right. Of course," I said. Secretly, though, I was sure Violet was just holding her cards close to the chest. She had to be thinking embezzling. But who would have found out about it and killed her? Her boss? It seemed unlikely; he was a marketing guy. He would just fire her. One of the owners? Someone who didn't want a scandal? I had no idea.

Fifteen minutes later I was standing in a spot of sun and enjoying the feeling of soaking up some vitamin D when Michaela, the receptionist, came out the back door.

"I can only stay out here for a minute," she said. "But I thought you should know. Lizzie had a spot of trouble with a man in marketing about eight months ago. Edgar was his name. He was about her age, divorced ages ago, and pretty creepy. He decided he wanted to have a go with Lizzie, but she wasn't interested. She was much too good for a sod like him anyway. Eventually he took things too far, she told him off and went to HR. Edgar was fired, but he swore before he left that he'd, and I quote, 'make that bitch pay.'"

"Wow," I said. "I wonder why Mr. Browning didn't tell us any of this. After all, if Edgar doesn't work for the company anymore, there can't have been any harm."

Michaela frowned. "Well for one thing, the

company really hushed it up. They didn't want it to get out, because it would be such a scandal. Edgar's last name is Enderby. He's one of the sons of the president of the company."

I inhaled sharply. Now there was a motive if I'd ever heard one.

Violet next to me frowned, however. "If he was the president's son, then why was he the one fired and not Dalton? After all, people like that are known to take care of their own."

"Lizzie had a video of the incident. She didn't trust Edgar at all, and whenever he came to her office she would turn the computer monitor's camera on and secretly record everything. She swore if they didn't fire him she'd release the video to the media. She said it in front of the whole office, so everyone knew. They had a meeting with everyone later, where we were all told to never say anything about it again, that it might cost us our jobs. But they did as she asked and fired Edgar. Anyway, I have to go. I can't be seen out here with you. That whole losing my job thing, you know?"

"Thank you for the information," Violet told her as Michaela nodded and slipped back into the building. Violet and I walked away in silence, each of us processing the information we'd just learned. This Edgar guy sounded like a real piece of work, and as far as I was concerned, he was now at the top of my suspect list.

CHAPTER 10

I wasn't entirely sure where we were walking to, but about half an hour after we left, we found ourselves in front of Violet's apartment.

"Oh," I said. "Sorry, I didn't realize you were going home."

"Ah, merde," she replied. "My apologies. I got so caught up in my thoughts, I forgot that you were there. But while we are here, I shall introduce you to your new landlady. After all, there is nothing we can do until tonight."

"What are we doing tonight?" I asked, slightly insulted at the fact that Violet had completely not realized that I'd followed her for a half hour walk around London.

"Something much more fun and interesting than anything you would be doing as a doctor," she replied cryptically. She led me further down the street, to number ten. The building was absolutely gorgeous. Painted in a light beige colour that suited it incredibly well, with white accents around the windows, the design was rather Edwardian, but still with a modern feel to it—the kind of feel you get when an old building with good bones has been renovated, but in a way that maintains the character of the old building. The main floor had a bay window that jutted out nicely, adding some depth to the building, and was surrounded by a fancy wrought-iron gate that made everything look a lot classier. At ground level, below the red clay steps leading up to the main house, was a door leading to what must be the apartment I was about to live in.

Violet climbed the steps and rang the bell. It took only a moment for the door to open. Mrs. Michaels was about four feet tall, thin as a rail, with an aged face but incredibly keen blue eyes. Her grey hair was neatly done up, and she was dressed as if she was going to church. If I had to guess, she had to be in her late eighties, but she moved like a woman thirty years younger.

"Ah, Violet. My favorite Frenchwoman! You know, if it were not because of your people, I would not have had to live through the bombings in London. You would think after the First World War, that the French would have learned. But ah! No. The Germans, they were also supposed to learn. Alas, they did not. Though I will say your Charlie there had more balls than our Neville Chamberlain. Why on earth anyone voted for that man is beyond me. Ah, this must be your new friend from America. Welcome!"

I couldn't help but smile at Mrs. Michaels. She obviously didn't fit the mold of the elderly woman who was too polite to ever have an opinion.

"Of course," she said to me, "There's a certain irony to people from your part of the world coming back to the motherland, after all those years. Your ancestors fought to get away from us, you know."

"I know," I replied with a bit of a smile. "My father was born in Scotland, however. His parents moved to America when he was a boy, but I do have a British passport."

"Ah, lovely. Not that passports should mean much these days anyway. Open borders for everyone, that's what I say. But these damn people voting to leave the EU. Farmers from up north, scared that a brown person might move in next to them, when the closest thing they've ever seen to an Arab is the postman whose family moved here from Italy three generations ago."

I wasn't sure if giggling was the appropriate reaction, but it was absolutely what I wanted to do. Mrs. Michaels had an opinion on everything, it seemed. And on the bright side, she wasn't a racist old person like my grandparents.

Mrs. Michaels positively bounded down the stairs with a key which she inserted into the lock in the apartment down below.

"Now, it's not the nicest flat," she told me. "But it's a decent enough place to live, and a good size for one." When we walked in, my mouth dropped open. The place was absolutely gorgeous! All the walls were painted white, except for the one on the left, which was a gorgeous robin's egg blue. The white couches were covered in matching blue blankets, with a couple of pillows embroidered with the Union Jack on the front. The kitchen took up most of the far wall, with stainless steel appliances, and in the far corner was a little table for two with a couple of cute chairs.

"Wow!" I said. "This is amazing!"

"Well thank you dear," Mrs. Michaels replied. "It didn't look like much a few years ago, but I thought to myself that I had to make it liveable, so I had everything changed up. I wasn't sure if I quite liked the modern look, but the young man in charge of construction told me it was all the rage."

"It looks incredible," I said, almost afraid to touch anything. I took my shoes off before continuing further inside along the light hardwood floors. Peeking into the bedroom, I saw it was painted in the same style, with one blue wall, and a nice, low queen-sized bed.

"Now, I hear you have a cat, is that correct?" Mrs. Michaels asked.

"It is; I hope that won't be a problem?" I was finding myself already getting attached to Biscuit.

"Oh no, of course not. So long as he's willing to

put up with some attention from a little old lady with a soft spot for animals."

"Of course," I replied. "He seems to be a sweet little thing."

"Oh, good. I take the same attitude with children as I do with cats: they're perfectly acceptable for small periods of time, so long as they go home with someone else afterwards."

I laughed at the joke. "So no children then?"

"Good God, no. Not that it was especially acceptable back in my day to have that attitude. We ended up telling people we were incapable of having children, then they suggested adoption. Can you imagine? The only thing worse than having your own children is having to raise someone else's. Absolutely not. That's the good thing about menopause. Everyone stops asking you when on earth you're going to procreate, as though that were the ultimate achievement a woman could aspire to."

I had a feeling Mrs. Michaels was an incredibly interesting woman.

"What did you do instead, then? What was your career?" I asked.

"Oh, I did a few things here and there while traveling with Tommy. We were very avid travelers back in the day." I had a sneaking suspicion Mrs. Michaels was deliberately avoiding the details.

"All right, well, you'll have to tell me all about it one day," I told her.

"I'll come down for tea one day then. Though I'll

warn you, it takes a few glasses of wine before I'm willing to spill the good stuff."

"Deal." I liked Mrs. Michaels. It seemed there was more to her than met the eye. No wonder Violet got along with her.

"Mrs. Michaels is underselling just how interesting her good stories are," Violet added from her spot in the corner. She seemed to be enjoying watching the interaction between us, and I turned to her.

"It sounds like you know a lot about Mrs. Michaels' life," I said.

"Well, she's kept me out of jail once or four times," Mrs. Michaels replied. Ok, I was definitely going to invite her over for tea and break out the wine.

"Now how much do I owe you for the flat?" I asked, half dreading the answer. A place like this could go for two thousand pounds a month, easily.

"Oh how about we call it one hundred a week?" Mrs. Michaels said. My heart stopped for a moment.

"I couldn't do that!" I replied. "That's far too little." I mean, a hundred a week was an absolutely amazing price, but it was practically robbery. I couldn't steal from a little old woman. If she'd doubled that price, that was the range I'd been looking at.

"A friend of Violet's is a friend of mine," she replied with a wink. "I know I could get more. Don't you worry yourself about me, dear, although I appreciate the sentiment. It's yours for a hundred."

"Thank you so much," I replied. Hey, if she insisted, I certainly wasn't going to say no.

"Now here's your key," she said, handing it to me. "Feel free to drop the rent off whenever, I'm just upstairs, as you know. If you need anything, I'm usually around," she said. "Except for Wednesday mornings. That's when I have my gymnastics class." I had no idea if she was joking or not, but I had a feeling she was telling the truth. She was the only octogenarian I knew who still did gymnastics.

"Thank you, I really appreciate it," I told her. "I'll stop by the bank on my way back with my things and have the first week's rent for you then."

"All right, dearie. You're a responsible one, aren't you? Excellent. Too many young people these days aren't responsible. Not that I begrudge them their fun. After all, you are only young once, and most people become boring when they are old. But that does not mean others do not depend on them. For example, if you are going to take the day off to do drugs in the park, have the decency to call in sick to work first."

I took the key and smiled as Mrs. Michaels headed back toward the door. What an incredible woman, I thought as Violet's phone rang. She answered it and slipped out the door in front of us. I led Mrs. Michaels back up to her home, though she refused my offer of a hand up the stairs—"I'm old, not disabled!"—and then headed back down to my new place just as Violet was hanging up the phone.

"Thank you for organizing this," I told her. "I mean that. This place is amazing."

"I thought you would like it. Now, I just got the phone call from Enderby Insurance, who are not going to allow us to see their financial records after all."

"Oh, no," I replied, but Violet just shrugged.

"The instant she was going to ask a committee I knew it was hopeless. Committees are useless for getting anything done. But that is not important. Instead, we go tonight to find the truth."

"Tonight? What are we doing?"

"We are going to get the files ourselves. I will be back here at one tomorrow morning, you had better have a nap before we go, as we will not be stopping for coffee on the way. Dress in black, but not suspiciously."

And with that, Violet headed back down to her own house, leaving me staring after her, and wondering if what we were going to be doing tonight was completely legal, because it certainly didn't sound that way.

CHAPTER 11

a s soon as I got back to the hostel I found Biscuit napping on my pillow, but as soon as he noticed he wasn't alone in the room anymore he jumped up and rubbed himself against my legs. What a little sweetie.

"I've got you a new home," I told him. "We're moving to Kensington, if you want to help me pack my things."

Of course, to Biscuit, "helping" mostly involved batting at my clothes as I tried to pack them into my backpack, lying down on my iPad and refusing to move—I figured he liked the heat—and then playing with the laces of my shoes as I tried to put them on. He calmed down as soon as I grabbed the harness and leash, however, and I gently stuck him in my purse for a minute while I left the hostel. I'd have to come back to check out later, as well as grab my bike which was still in the room, but that was all right—I'd already paid for the week so I had a few days left in my room. In a way it was a little bit sad that I could fit everything I owned, and everything I needed for Biscuit, into my one backpack and a couple of shopping bags, but I also knew that now that I had my own place I'd be able to start buying things to really make it my own.

Since I wasn't sure what the protocol was for taking a cat on the subway—and because I was still very self-conscious about walking a cat through the streets of London—I opted to splurge on a cab ride to Kensington. Ten minutes later Biscuit was happily sniffing every corner of our new home as I unpacked my meagre belongings.

"Look at this, little guy. We're moving up in the world."

Biscuit meowed at me happily, playing with my sock for a moment before being distracted by the tiniest ball of fluff in the corner and pouncing on his new prey.

My stomach began to growl, but at the same time, I kind of just wanted to settle into my new place. I grabbed my iPad and ordered take-out from a place nearby, the site promising me that in fifteen minutes I'd have some nice butter chicken and rice. Sure enough, exactly fourteen minutes later there was a knock at my door, and I dove into the comfort food —Biscuit begging for bits of chicken while I turned on the TV. I laughed at the rerun of a celebrity talk show called The Graham Norton Show, who actually had some pretty big celebrities on—this one had Matt Damon, Novak Djokovic the tennis player, an English singer who I didn't recognize and Martin Freeman. Eventually I fell asleep, wondering what on earth Violet had planned for that night.

* * *

AT TEN THIRTY I was looking at my wardrobe, trying to find as many dark clothes as possible. I eventually settled on the closest thing I had to all black: very dark blue skinny jeans, a black turtleneck, and a scarf to hide my auburn hair. Luckily I did have some black flats, and coupled with black socks I figured it was good enough. Looking at myself in the mirror, I sighed. Even to me I looked shifty and suspicious. Still, it was what Violet had said to wear.

When she knocked on my door at eleven, she was dressed pretty similarly to me, carrying a small purse that I had a feeling had more than just some makeup for touch-ups. She didn't say much; evidently she was thinking about what we were about to do. Hailing a cab, she had the driver drop us off at my old hostel.

"Why are we here?" I asked as she paid the fare.

"Because we have a reason for being here. You still technically live here, remember? We have a plausible reason to be at your place after midnight, we don't have a good reason to be at Enderby Insurance."

"So that means whatever we're about to do isn't exactly legal, right?" I asked.

"I asked you to dress in black for a midnight excursion to an office where everyone went home at five. Did you really think there was going to be anything legal about this?"

I had to be honest: deep down, I knew this was totally going to be illegal. I just hadn't let myself admit it. I swallowed hard and steeled myself for what we were going to do next. "Come on, we're casually going to walk toward the Enderby building," Violet told me, and we strode down the street together.

I was completely and totally torn here. On the one hand, I didn't want to commit a crime! I had always been a good girl. The worst thing I'd ever done was jaywalk, and maybe drove a little bit too fast from time to time. But whatever we were doing, it was going to be worse than that. I had a feeling this was breaking and entering territory. But at the same time, I couldn't deny a part of me was excited. For the first time since my accident, I could feel the rush of adrenaline coursing through me. I was part of something bigger than me. I was helping to find a killer, even if I was just mostly tagging along. So what if it wasn't exactly legal? There's that saying about having to break a few eggs to make an omelette, isn't there? That totally applied to this situation.

At the same time, I was all too conscious of the

fact that Violet thought I was a terrible liar. The last thing I wanted to do was to screw this up, to make her think that this was all a mistake and taking me with her was a terrible idea. So I took a deep breath and tried my best to relax as we walked through the streets toward Enderby Insurance. Every time a car drove slowly past I was sure it was a cop, but I forced myself to stay relaxed and not turn around to check each time I heard an engine coming near us.

After what seemed like an eternity, but in reality had only been ten minutes, we were in front of the Enderby Insurance building. Rather than going to the front door, however, Violet walked past it and toward the entrance for the underground parking area.

"They only man the underground parking until eleven pm," she explained to me. "Afterwards they have a single security guard to watch over four floors of cars, and some CCTV cameras. Be careful to follow me exactly."

Violet moved like a cat, and I found that I had trouble keeping up with her. She entered the underground garage on the far side, away from the unmanned guard's hut. She stopped about fifteen feet past it, and took five confident strides, ending up right in between an entrance lane and an exit lane. She walked directly on the center line for a little while before stopping and moving to the far wall, pressing herself against it, then edging her way carefully toward a little enclave. When I entered the enclave a few seconds after her, she smiled.

"Not too bad at all. Good work."

The praise affected me more than I'd like to admit. It was like getting a compliment from a professor, I realized, and blushed slightly. There was a door in the enclave, a thick one. Violet took some tools out from the small purse she was carrying, and began to pick at the lock. A minute later, I heard a click and Violet opened the door a fraction of an inch, but no more.

"There will be a guard stationed on the ground floor. I doubt there will be more, but all the same, we have to be careful." She slipped the door open and looked out, then motioned for me to follow her inside.

My heart was pounding in my chest. I'd never done anything like this before. When I was in the sixth grade, I was hanging out with some friends one night and they decided to see if we could climb onto the roof of the elementary school near our house—spoiler alert: we couldn't—but it had been the biggest rush of my young life to worry about breaking the rules and being caught doing something we weren't supposed to be doing.

This gave me that same kind of rush. Unfortunately, now as a thirty-year-old, I was well aware that this rush could very well lead to serious jail time if it went wrong, as opposed to the severe threat of being grounded for a month back in grade six. Violet crept up the stairs like a cat; she was stealthy. Quick, but quiet as a mouse. When we reached the door for the ground floor, she knelt underneath the small window looking out into the building's lobby. Taking out her phone, Violet subtly moved the camera up into the window area, took a photo, and had a look. Clever; there was only about an inch of phone sticking up in the window. Not only would the guard not have noticed that little movement, but unless he had eyes like a hawk he wouldn't have noticed the camera sticking up for a split second.

She nodded. "He is at his desk. We're all good. Follow me."

The part I hadn't realized was that by taking the stairs and not the elevator, which would have been closed for the night by now, on top of being right next to where the guard was sitting, Violet's plan involved climbing eleven more flights of stairs, with only the light from her phone to guide us. I normally didn't make a big deal out of my knee; other than the slight limp I was mostly stuck with, I barely ever felt anything out of the ordinary anymore. But today, by the time we finished climbing all of those steps, my knee was definitely aching. Not to mention I was incredibly out of breath, since it wasn't as if I was hitting the gym every day since my accident. Most of my physiotherapy had been designed to rebuild the muscle in my leg after the surgery; my cardio was definitely lacking.

"You need to ride that bicycle more often," Violet

teased gently. Of course she wasn't the least bit out of breath. Some things just weren't fair.

"Give me a minute," I asked, my hands on my knees, breathing hard, and Violet did as requested. "Where are we, anyway?" I asked.

"We're on the floor below where we were today, at the stairwell next to the elevators. As soon as I open this door, we have sixty seconds to figure out the code for the alarm before the police are called."

"And how exactly do you plan to do that?" I asked.

"With a little bit of thinking," Violet replied. A minute later she asked if I was ok. I nodded, and she opened the door, striding straight to the little white box next to the elevators blinking away. If I thought I was tense before, it was nothing like having a definite timeline.

I watched as Violet looked at the numbers on the keypad. God, they all looked exactly the same to me. How on earth was she going to figure out the code? She tried a four-digit combination. Nothing happened, the light continued blinking. Oh God. This was going to fail. The cops were going to be called, we were going to be arrested, I was going to jail and then when I was done serving my sentence I was going to be deported back to America. This was such a horrible idea. Maybe I still had time to run out of here, run back down the stairs and get out. I was just about to start panicking for real when Violet punched in another set of four numbers. This time, the light stopped blinking and turned solid green.

I froze where I was, staring at it. Green was good, right? Violet turned to me, a grin on her face.

"See? Easy."

Yeah, easy. I was pretty sure my lifespan had just been shortened by at least five years.

"How did you know the code?" I asked, and Violet motioned me over.

"See the keypad? Look at the numbers." I looked at them, but nothing stood out to me. There were all the numbers from zero to nine. Well, except for the four, which had been kind of smudged out.

"Oh!" I exclaimed, suddenly realizing what Violet wanted me to see. "Some of the numbers have been worn down, which means they've been tapped the most."

"*Exactement*," Violet exclaimed happily. "It is exactly that. So now you see, the four numbers of the code for the alarm system—I recognize the company, I know their codes are four numbers and none of the numbers are used twice—are four, two, six and eight. Humans are creatures that like patterns, so it is most likely the four that is the first number in the code, as we write from the left to the right, and the four is the number furthest to the left. The shape is most likely a diamond, so the question becomes: 'is the code four, eight, six, two or four, two, six, eight'? It could be others, of course, but always try the most obvious combination first. It turned out that it was the second option. four, two, six, eight was the code."

Enough light poured through the windows from

the city lights below that we were able to see just well enough to make our way through the offices without further help from the phone flashlight. Violet put it away as we headed down a hallway.

"How do you know there isn't any extra security? Cameras and stuff?" I asked in a whisper, wondering if I should cover my face just in case.

"I looked at the security the last few times we were here. The first thing you should always do when you enter a building is determine how to get in unnoticed, in case the need arises."

"Between this and telling me to practice lying, I'm starting to wonder if you really do work with the police, or if you're the reason bodies are popping up everywhere," I muttered as Violet stopped in front of a solid door. I had no idea what was on the other side of it, but she evidently did.

"The line between solving crimes and committing them is very thin," she replied. That explained why I was standing in the middle of an office hallway after midnight wondering if I was going to wake up in jail the next day. She took her pickpocketing tools back out of her bag and a moment later she opened the door.

"Wait," she told me before going in. Slipping a mirror from her pocket, Violet checked something on the other side of the door.

"Good. No cameras, we are clear," she said, entering the room. I couldn't help but notice that she checked once more once we were in the room to ensure there weren't any other cameras around.

"The good thing about major companies is they never think that their servers can be touched. They always think technology will be magically protected," she said as she made her way expertly between racks of computer hardware. Pulling an eleven-inch laptop from her purse, along with a cable, Violet plugged it expertly into a certain hole in the server room.

"This will take some time," she told me. "Likely around twenty, thirty minutes."

I looked as Violet tapped away at the screen.

"So you're good with computers, hey?" I asked.

"You could say that, yes."

"How good, exactly? Like, are you a hacker?"

"Hacker is a very broad term. But yes, in general, I am very good at getting into technology that is generally protected. As you must imagine, I did not have many friends growing up. However, the computer, it was an escape. An excellent escape. I am more comfortable with my computer than with people."

I could understand that, for sure.

"Is the alarm disabled for the whole office?" I asked. Violet nodded. "It should be, yes."

"Can you pick the lock upstairs for me? I want to have another look at Elizabeth's office. After all, there isn't much for me to do here while we wait for the computer."

"Excellent idea," Violet replied. "Give me three

minutes to set everything up, and I will come with you."

The three minutes felt like an eternity. I knew that Violet had disabled the alarm. I'd seen her do it. And after all, we'd been here for minutes already. If anything had been triggered, at the very least that guard would have come upstairs to see what had happened. But there was still that little niggly part of my brain that knew what we were doing was a serious crime and couldn't help but expect the police to break the door down and arrest us at any moment.

Still, we made our way back to the doorway, then upstairs to the floor where Elizabeth Dalton worked with no issues. And sure enough, when we entered, the light on the alarm system box was a solid green. We were all good.

Silently, Violet and I made our way down the hall. I couldn't help but think of how creepy this place was. It was dark; I could make out the silhouette of Violet in front of me, and I could tell where the walls were, but not much more than that. The HVAC system hummed low in the background, but apart from that there was silence. It felt like the beginning of a horror movie, when you just know something's going to come out from one of the rooms and murder you.

I was so caught up in my thoughts that I didn't notice Violet stop in front of me, and when I walked into her my heart leapt into my throat. I jumped about three feet in the air and let out the first part of a squeal, which I quickly stopped by clamping my hand over my mouth.

"Just a little bit jumpy?" Violet asked softly. She had stopped in front of Elizabeth Dalton's door. We were here.

"Sorry," I murmured, my heart pounding so hard in my chest I was sure Violet could hear it.

"It is all right, you get used to committing crimes after a while. It is the worst part, really. It is not good to get complacent. A close call now and then—how do you say—keeps you on your toes."

"Well, I'll be perfectly happy if that close call doesn't come tonight," I said as I heard the click of the lock. We entered the office, both of us pulling out our phones. It was obviously too risky to turn the light on in here, so we took out the flashlights.

Violet made her way to the filing cabinet and opened the top shelf, taking out a number of plain off-white folders. She handed me half the pile.

Years of being a medical student meant that I was fully used to studying texts late at night, and my old habits came back to me pretty quickly. I settled myself down on the floor, the stack of files next to me, and began to flip through them while Violet did the same at the table.

"Are we looking for anything in particular?" I asked.

"Keep an open mind. You never know what could be important, but you also do not want to direct your thoughts in a single direction. That is dangerous, you may overlook a vital piece of information if it does not fit the narrative you have formed in your head."

"Got it," I replied. It seemed like my files were basically just invoices from a number of companies – mainly printers, ad agencies, TV stations and other marketing-related businesses—that Elizabeth Dalton was in charge of paying. It quickly became apparent that keeping an open mind wasn't going to be a problem; keeping an interested mind was. But hey, if I could make it through a class entirely dedicated to the internal structure of the human eye, surely I could flip through some invoices and make sure nothing was off about them.

Fifteen minutes later I was flipping through my fourth folder of boring invoices, and the only conclusion I'd come to was that marketing services were a *very* lucrative business. Tens of thousands of pounds per month just to advertise the business on Facebook? Maybe I'd just found my new career path. I was flipping through the invoices when suddenly something caught my eye. Stuck to the back of one of the pieces of paper was about half a post-it note. It was the same colour as the paper, and obviously didn't belong.

Pulling it off the page, I had a look at the note. It just had some stuff scribbled on it that didn't make much sense to me:

14-1: 1,000
28-1: 1,000
10-2: 1,000

. . .

08-6

Anything else that might have been on the post-it had since disappeared.

"Hey Violet," I told her, calling her over. "I think I might have found something. I don't know. It's weird."

She came over and looked at the note.

"Well now that *is* interesting," Violet said as she looked at the note carefully. "I don't think Elizabeth Dalton was embezzling money from the company anymore. I think she was blackmailing someone."

CHAPTER 12

"*B*lackmailing someone?" I asked. "How do you know?"

"I'm fairly certain the numbers at the bottom are the first half of a sort code, which has been cut off. The numbers at the top look like a date, and an amount. Perhaps how much a person is supposed to pay, and into which account. Is the other half of the note in here somewhere?"

We spent another half hour looking through all the files, but didn't come up with the other half of the note. Violet finally sat back on her heels, defeated. "Well, I cannot say I am very surprised. I expect Elizabeth Dalton tore the whole note in half, and must have thought she had thrown out both halves. It is only good fortune that one half escaped the bin."

"She really didn't seem to me to be the blackmailing type," I muttered to myself.

"There is never a type!" Violet admonished. "I doubt you would believe your new landlady to be the 'type' to smuggle one of the world's biggest sapphires into England, either."

"Wait, she did that?" I asked, my mouth dropping open.

"You will have to ask her," Violet replied. No wonder Mrs. Michaels could afford that amazing Kensington townhouse! "Now, I believe with this we are finished here. We will go back downstairs, we will get back the laptop, and we will go back home."

In all the excitement of actually finding a clue, for a moment I'd completely forgotten that we were still definitely not supposed to be here.

"Ok," I replied, and we put everything back in the filing cabinets as we found it—or as close to it as possible, anyway. Five minutes later we were back downstairs, unplugging Violet's laptop from the computer it was plugged into.

"The information I have here is likely worth millions of pounds," she told me. "And yet they still think a simple security system is completely fine. *Ils sont des idiots.* If I were a criminal, London would be the easiest target ever."

"You seem to have done all right for yourself on the side of the angels," I told her.

"It is true. Besides, I do not care about the money, for me it is the art of the problem," she replied, slipping the laptop back into her bag. Still, I saw her shake her head in disgust slightly as she locked the door back up after her. Evidently the computer genius in Violet wasn't content with the lack of adequate security in their server room.

We were walking back toward the door we had entered from next to the receptionist's desk when suddenly Violet grabbed me and pulled me down behind the receptionist's desk. I fell to the ground with a thud and was about to ask her what the hell she was doing when I saw Violet crouching next to me with a finger on her lips. I was obviously supposed to be quiet. I nodded my understanding. My heart pounded in my chest. Violet wasn't the type of person to scare someone just for the hell of it, I didn't think.

She motioned for me to look carefully out from the side of the desk with her, and I did. Looking at the door that led to the stairwell, a face suddenly passed by the small rectangular window in the door. It was the guard from downstairs. He peered through the window into the offices quickly, then kept going.

"Oh my God," I whispered about a minute later, when I finally dared to speak again. "He would have looked right at us." My heart pounded in my chest. I had never considered that I might die of a heart attack so young before tonight. "How on earth did you know he was coming?" I asked. Violet pointed to her ears.

"When you are in the habit of breaking into places, you learn to keep your senses on high alert."

"Remind me to bring you along whenever I

commit felonies," I told her. "Can we go out the other stairwell, the one with the door that leads right outside?"

Violet shook her head. "No, the door we came in from is the only door exiting the building that isn't alarmed, other than the front door, which is out for obvious reasons. We will wait for ten minutes, for the guard to finish his rounds, and then we will go back downstairs."

Those ten minutes were the longest of my life. I huddled under the desk, constantly terrified that the guard would come in, or notice the green light of the alarm system, and that we'd be caught. You know how people always use the phrase *worst case scenario?* Well, that phrase is a lie, because after that night, I was well aware that there was not simply one worst case scenario, there were dozens of them. And they all ran through my head while we waited.

After what felt like an eternity, Violet tapped my arm.

"I think we are probably safe to go now," she said.

"I don't like that use of the word 'probably'," I mumbled in reply, getting up. My legs were cramped from being stuck under that desk for so long, and I silently cursed my unfit, aging body. Two minutes later, however, Violet had re-armed the alarm system and we were both in the stairwell. This time around I was all too aware of just how much noise my feet made. To my ears, I sounded like an elephant pounding down the stairs. Surely the guard could hear, and would come flying back up the stairs to arrest us.

But, much to my surprise, we actually made it to the basement level fine, and a few minutes later had reversed our route around the security cameras and were back out in the street.

Believe me, I had never been so happy to feel the cool breeze of two am on my face.

"Come on," Violet said, leading me away. "We have done good work tonight."

"I hope so, because I think it cost me about ten years of my life," I replied, and Violet laughed.

"You are the one who wanted adventure."

"I always considered adventure to be more along the lines of not knowing what I ordered in a restaurant because it was in a foreign language, or getting on the wrong bus. Not breaking into a major insurance company in the middle of the night and stealing all of their financial data."

"You say tomato, I say to-mah-to," Violet said, and this time it was my turn to laugh. Laughing was a lot easier when you were fairly certain you weren't about to be thrown in jail for the rest of your life.

We took a taxi back to Kensington, where Violet bade me goodnight.

I slipped back into my new apartment, where Biscuit had happily settled himself to sleep on top of the covers on my bed. I watched him for a moment, then had a quick shower. By the time I got out, the adrenaline of the night was beginning to wear off, and I was asleep as soon as my head hit the pillow.

CHAPTER 13

I woke up the next morning to what felt like a massage. A massage with a lot of howling involved.

"Urrrggh," I said as I realized what was happening: Biscuit was kneading my back and making a racket. I was lying on my stomach, still half asleep, as my cat kneaded and howled at me to get up.

"Whaddayawann?" I asked, rolling over and looking at Biscuit. He reached up with a paw and booped me on the nose, then leapt deftly off the bed and stood in the doorway, looking back at me.

I had a sneaking suspicion I was late in serving breakfast. Grabbing my phone off the nightstand, I had a look at the time. It was just after eight, which meant I had been asleep for a little under five hours. Great. If there was one thing being an invalid with no job had led to, it was copious amounts of sleeping. I was definitely going to need a nap later on today.

I forced myself to roll out of bed and wandered into the kitchen area, where Biscuit was politely sitting next to his food bowl, waiting for breakfast.

"Sure, you look all nice and polite *now*," I muttered groggily to the cat as I got out a container of his food. I poured it into the bowl and he happily began eating it. I quietly bemoaned my lack of foresight in not buying any food for myself the day before. All I wanted to do was crawl back into my bed and sleep for another three hours, at least. Food could wait; if I was sleeping, I wouldn't be able to feel my hunger.

Just then, my phone buzzed. Great. If it was Violet, I was half tempted to pretend I was still asleep.

It was her, but luckily, she wasn't asking for anything.

Have given the info on the routing number to DCI Williams. Will text when I get information back.

Perfect! This meant I could absolutely crawl back into bed and get a few more hours in before there was anything to do. I made my way back to bed, and Biscuit followed me, content now that he was fed. Ten minutes later we were both dead to the world.

* * *

WHEN I WOKE UP AGAIN, just after noon, I forced myself to get out of bed, put some decent clothes on, and finally go find some food. I ended up at the

McDonalds across the street from the High Street Kensington underground station. What? After a night like the one I'd just had, quite frankly, I deserved a cheeseburger combo.

I had finished eating my meal and was sitting at the table, just beginning to regret my life choices when I got a text from Violet. She'd gotten the info from DCI Williams. I told her I could meet her at the police station, and she agreed. Since the Edgware Road underground station was just four stops away from Kensington, I crossed the street and hopped onto the next train heading northeast. Ten minutes later I was standing outside the police station where all this had started when Violet got out of a cab that pulled up in front of the station.

She looked so perfectly made up, like she'd gotten a great night's sleep—it was absolutely amazing. I was sure I was standing there with patches of hair still sticking out from when I rushed to brush it before leaving. I was wearing sunglasses to hide the dark circles under my eyes, and I hadn't realized until I left the apartment that I wasn't even wearing matching socks. How Violet managed to look that perfect after the night we had was beyond me completely.

Violet smiled a hello and we went into the police station. Going back up to the second floor, I saw DCI Williams sitting at a desk about halfway down the room. Cops milled around; everyone was obviously busy with work. DCI Williams saw us and waved us over; he was on the phone and he didn't look happy. As we got to the edge of the desk, he hung up, and handed a folder over to Violet.

"There's the information you asked for," he told her. "I don't think you'll get what you wanted out of it though. She had money in the house, sure, but not too much apart from that. We looked into it; apparently there was a will, her sister-in-law's son is the sole beneficiary. He's a bit of a loser, one of those kids who never really figured out what he wanted to do with his life. Lives in a council flat out in the east end, and by all accounts spends his dole cheque on video games. He's certainly not paying his rent with it. Anyway, we think he killed her for the house. We're going to bring him in later today."

"Congratulations," Violet told him. "You took the information I gave you and came to the wrong conclusion completely."

DCI Williams' face turned a little bit irritable. "So you think you know better who did it, then?" he asked.

"Of course. In fact, seeing this list, I know exactly who it was."

"And I suppose you're not going to tell me straight up."

"Seeing as you believe it was the nephew, it is obvious to me that you need your criminals handed to you on a platter, as you say in English. I will bring you your murderer, and it will be with a solid enough case that even you police will not be able to mess it up."

"Have you ever considered that maybe we're right and you're wrong?" DCI Williams asked.

"No," Violet replied confidently, and I raised my hand to my mouth to hide a smile.

"Well, we will see. I think you might find that your lack of faith in the Metropolitan Police is perhaps misplaced."

"Assuming the worst of the police force's detective skills has never led me astray yet. Thank you for the information," Violet said, holding up the folders.

"Yes, I can tell you're incredibly grateful," DCI Williams replied, shaking his head. I gave him a sympathetic smile and he nodded at me as I followed Violet back out of the police station. Violet was already reading through the file she'd been given. She started walking down the street, and a part of me wondered where we were headed, until we got to a little park next to a church about a block away from the police station. Violet settled herself on the bench and finished reading the pieces of paper in the file, passing them over to me when she was done.

The first few pieces of paper were a list of banks. It seemed it was all the banks with a sort code that started with the numbers 08-6. There were about forty of them. Great. It seemed every bank in England used a sort code that started with those three digits.

Unity Trust. The Co-Operative Bank. Citibank.

Northern Rock. Investec. Chelsea Building Society. The list went on and on.

The next sheet was a list of the various bank accounts Elizabeth Dalton had held. She certainly did have a lot of them, that was for sure. Four credit cards, with Visa, MasterCard and Amex, a savings account with Barclays, an investment account with Lloyds, checking accounts with Barclays and Virgin Money, a small mortgage with Barclays and a small personal loan with Citibank. For a woman who only really had one asset and not a ton of money otherwise, she certainly had a number of accounts. I wondered if perhaps the number of credit lines had gotten to her, and that was the reason for the black-mailing.

After the list was a printout of the statements of all her accounts. The chequing accounts were virtu-ally empty, the credit cards maxed out, and the personal loan nowhere near being paid off. It seemed Elizabeth Dalton lived very much paycheck to paycheck. She didn't exactly have the day-to-day finances of a person able to afford all the pretty toys she was buying. I had a feeling Violet was right about the blackmail.

"So how do we figure out who she was blackmail-ing?" I asked. "I mean, she had to have *something* on someone at the bank. The question is, who. We find that out, we find the murderer."

Violet smiled at me. "That's the more difficult way to get around it. After all, think of the people we have already met or know of at Enderby Insurance. You have Edgar Enderby, for one. She could have been blackmailing his father; telling him that if he didn't pay her off, she would go to the police."

"So he must be the prime suspect!" I said. Violet just smiled, then continued.

"But you also have her boss, Leo Browning. He's cheating on his wife."

"What? How could you *possibly* know that?" I asked.

"The first time we met him, Leo Browning was wearing a navy blue suit with a pastel pink shirt underneath. The head of marketing of a major insurance firm would know better than to color co-ordinate that badly, which meant he had no other choice. That meant he did not go home the previous night, and had to change into an extra shirt that he would keep at work, as do most executives."

"But maybe he just stayed late at the office the night before?"

"Maybe, but his hands were covered in the lotion that they use at the Ritz Hotel, I could smell it when he shook my hand. And just in case that doesn't fully convince you, did you notice him in the background of one of the Christmas party photos? No? Well, if you look closely, he has his hand resting on the bottom of a long-haired blonde woman. There were a few long blonde hairs on his jacket. She is the woman he's having an affair with."

"So then it's between Browning and Enderby's father."

"You're forgetting Browning's head of advertising that we met, Jennifer Ashton. She's a high functioning alcoholic."

"I'm almost afraid to ask how you could possibly know that."

"You noticed the half-empty container of mints and the antacids on her desk? She eats the mints like candy, and takes the antacid for the stomach pains she's getting from taking in that much alcohol. Did you notice the spider angioma on her neck?"

"Yes, of course. I assumed it was simply because of birth control pills, since she didn't look pregnant. But I suppose you're right, it can be a sign of overconsumption of alcohol. I guess I just assumed that someone that high up in a major corporation wouldn't be a high-functioning alcoholic. I know, I know, never assume anything," I said as Violet opened her mouth. I hadn't realized just how much I assumed about people.

"Fine, so we have a few suspects," I said.

"I'm not finished, either. The receptionist, Michaela, has been stealing things from the office, probably to resell."

At this point, I just trusted that Violet was telling the truth. My heart sunk at the realization that there were a *lot* of people in that office with secrets. "Great. So basically we're no closer to finding out who Elizabeth Dalton blackmailed than before."

"That's not true at all. I know exactly who she was blackmailing, and who the most likely murderer is."

"What? How? Who is it?"

"Leo Browning, her boss."

"You're making that up. Surely you have to be making that up."

"Did you look at the list of bank codes I gave you? And at the bank accounts Elizabeth Dalton owned?"

"Yes."

"Did any of them match?"

I had to admit, I hadn't thought of that. I scanned through both lists again quickly.

"Well there's the loan with Citibank but she wouldn't get a blackmailer to pay her loan directly… Oh!" I cried, seeing it. "There! Virgin Money."

"*Exactement*. She was getting the blackmailer to pay into her Virgin Money account. There are only a few pounds in the account right now, because she had spent nearly all of the money, but if you go back you can see deposits of thousands of pounds at a time. And some of the dates and numbers correspond with what was found on the post-it note."

"Ok, I get that. But none of that explains why Leo Browning is the one responsible."

Violet smiled. "Ah, but the thing you do not realize is that *you* are the reason I know. Do you not remember when you asked to borrow his pen?"

Realization dawned upon me. The Virgin Money pen.

"The pen!"

"Yes, the pen. Virgin Money is a bank of the working class. And besides, they have only six branches in London, they are not a large bank. It is highly unlikely that a man in Browning's position would come about having a pen of that sort unless he was in one of the branches and took it back with him inadvertently. The only reason he would be in such a bank would be to pay Dalton's ransom, as he would be the type of man to do private banking. He would have wanted to make a cash deposit so as to leave no paper trail for his wife to find."

I nodded slowly as the realization dawned upon me. "So now we know who the murderer is!"

"We do."

"So we have to go back and tell DCI Williams, before he brings in the nephew."

Violet shook her head. "No, not yet. After all, there is evidence of blackmail here. There is no evidence of murder. I suggest we go and speak with Mr. Browning once again. We are only a few minutes from the office, after all."

CHAPTER 14

y heart raced as we approached the Enderby Insurance offices. For one thing, around twelve hours ago I'd broken into this building and stolen super secret information. The memory of that was still way too fresh in my brain to be perfectly calm about it. And for another, I knew we were going up to confront a murderer.

This time we walked in through the front door and took the elevator up to the offices. Michaela greeted us brightly at the entrance.

"Hello, have you solved the murder yet?" she asked us.

"Possibly. You will know in a couple of days," Violet told her reassuringly.

"Oh good. I've been feeling so bad for poor Lizzie. No one deserves to die like that."

"I agree," I told her. I couldn't believe a nice girl

like her could be stealing things from the office. But then, Violet seemed to have perfect explanations for everything else.

"Are you here to look at her office again?" Michaela asked, getting up.

"We were actually hoping to speak with Mr. Browning if he's available."

"Oh all right, let me have a look," she said, sitting back down. "I believe his new secretary is being hired soon. That will be nice, as I've been having to do Lizzie's old duties as well as my own for the last few days. It looks as though he's in a meeting, but if you want to have a seat I can probably fit you in for a couple of minutes afterwards, in about a quarter of an hour?"

"That's fine," Violet told her, and we made our way to the couches to wait for our appointment with a murderer.

"What are we going to do when we get in there?" I asked.

"Just follow my lead."

"That's code for you have no idea, isn't it?"

Violet simply smiled in return. I was half teasing her; Violet seemed to know exactly what she was doing at any given moment. But somehow, I couldn't help but bet there was a bit of truth to the statement. How do you get a murderer to confess to a crime if you're not a cop?

I supposed I was about to find out. Michaela came out and led us into Leo Browning's office. She knocked twice on the door, quick, efficient raps, then opened it and let us in. Leo Browning was sitting at his desk, signing a piece of paper. He looked up and smiled at us.

"Ladies, welcome back. I'm afraid I only have a few minutes, but please, anything I can do to help find Elizabeth's killer."

"For one thing, you can tell us how much she took you for when she was blackmailing you."

Browning's face immediately fell. The jovial, slightly pink tinge to his hue disappeared completely as he paled.

"I don't know what you're talking about. I'm not being blackmailed at all."

"Really? So if we go to the Virgin Money branch in the city centre and ask for their security cameras from three twelve pm last Monday, you won't appear on them, depositing money into Elizabeth Dalton's bank account?" Violet asked.

Browning seemed to realize then that the game was up. His shoulders drooped and he sighed loudly, opening his hands as if in defeat.

"All right. You have me. I haven't broken any laws. I am being blackmailed, although I won't tell you what for."

"You've been cheating on your wife with a woman that you meet at the Ritz," Violet replied, and any color that might have remained in Leo Browning's face disappeared completely.

"Fine. But please, what I tell you, it has to stay

between us. I was being blackmailed. For about six, maybe seven months now. You think it was my secretary who was blackmailing me?"

"We know it was her. You didn't?"

Leo Browning shrugged, stiffly. "I had my suspicions. After all, she was the one who answered my phone calls. She read all my mail. She had access to most of my emails. I tried to be discreet, but if there was one person in the office who might have figured it out, it was most likely her. But you're wrong. It wasn't Elizabeth."

"We have very, very solid evidence that it was."

"And I have very, very solid evidence that it wasn't." He tapped away at his computer for a moment, then turned the screen toward us. Violet and I leaned forward slightly to read it.

It was an email, and looking at the date, Browning had received it the day before, just after eleven am. It came from an anonymous e-mail address, zzthjslfcic-cu@hotmail.com. I knew instinctively it would be completely untraceable. My eyes dropped below to read the text of the email.

If you don't want your wife to find out about your affair, continue your regular deposits into the following account:

Sort code 08-61-15 Account Number 0026547

"Do you have any copies of the old ransom letters?" Violet asked immediately. I was trying to remember, I was fairly certain the sort code was the same as the one for Elizabeth Dalton's bank account, but something about the account number seemed off.

"No, I destroyed them all, sorry," Browning replied. "You can understand, of course."

Violet only nodded, her brow furrowed in thought. "This changes things," she said, almost to herself.

"Changes what?" Browning asked, and a moment later his eyebrows rose and his eyes widened. "Oh!" he exclaimed, coming to the realization of why we were here. "You thought *I* had killed Elizabeth!"

"I'm still not sure you haven't," Violet said. "After all, if you had suspected she was your blackmailer, you could still have killed her to get rid of her."

"No," Leo Browning said. "No, I suspected her, but I had no proof. I'm not a murderer, either way."

"Do you have proof of that?"

"In fact I do! I was called away on business at the last second the morning Elizabeth was killed. I left for Manchester ninety minutes before Elizabeth went on break."

"I assume you have proof of this?"

"Of course!" Leo Browning pulled out his phone and tapped away for a minute, before handing it to Violet. "Here is my ticket for the train. And Michaela should have my receipt for the taxi I took from the station to the office I was going to, about two and a half hours after the train left." Violet nodded slowly, then handed Leo Browning back his phone.

"You were an absolutely perfect suspect," Violet

told him, standing up. "But, luckily for you, you do have an alibi. I will be checking up on it. Let me ask you one more question: did anything change about the threats at any point in the past, or were they always exactly the same?"

Browning thought to himself for just a moment before answering. "Yes, yes there was a change," he said. "About one month after the threats began. Whoever it was had started off by asking for small amounts. A couple of hundred pounds every few weeks. But then, suddenly, they changed to one thousand, and it's been one thousand a fortnight ever since."

"Thank you, Mr. Browning," Violet said, leaving.

"Wait, you're not going to tell my wife anything, are you?" Leo Browning asked as we left the room, pleading in his voice. Violet didn't reply.

"Are you going to tell his wife?" I asked her. I honestly didn't know what to expect.

"No. I have no reason to. But that does not mean he does not deserve to sweat a little bit over it all the same."

I smiled slightly to myself. Violet stopped at the reception desk and asked Michaela for the receipt. Her eyes widened.

"Oh, you don't think Mr. Browning did it, do you?" she asked in a hushed voice.

"If you have the receipt, it pretty well proves he couldn't have," Violet replied.

"Good. I couldn't possibly believe it would be anyone who works here."

"Well, Michaela, I can tell you with almost complete certainty that it is someone who works here," Violet replied, and we left and made our way back to the elevator as the receptionist's eyes widened to the size of saucers.

"So what happens now?" I asked. "Something's weird about this."

"Something is weird about this. How do you feel about eating some lunch?"

I wasn't exceptionally hungry, but I agreed to the meal, mainly because I could get away with just having a smoothie at whatever new age health food place Violet decided to take us to. To my chagrin, it was the same place as that first breakfast.

We sat down at a booth and Violet began speaking before we even had menus handed to us.

"We know that the money went to Elizabeth Dalton. The bank account is in her name. There is no other way she could have got the money, and no other way to explain how she could afford the luxuries in her home."

"And yet she's dead, and Browning is still being blackmailed."

"*Précisement.* What do you make of that, Cassie?" Violet asked me. I closed my eyes and tried to think things through.

"Well, the obvious answer that can be ruled out is ghosts," I started.

"Yes, let us assume that the paranormal is not involved in this crime," Violet replied, and I could practically feel her rolling her eyes at me.

"One thing that I noticed was that Browning said that he had 'destroyed' the previous notes. That means that this is the first one he had received by email. Which means something else has changed."

"*Oui!* Yes, that is good! Excellent deducting. You are getting better." I smiled at the praise.

"Something has changed. I think that someone *else* is blackmailing Browning, but what I don't know is how they would have found out he was being blackmailed in the first place. Or what their link to Dalton was."

"Very good," Violet replied, nodding. A waiter came over and handed us a couple menus, but I was too engrossed in the conversation to even bother looking at it.

"You know, obviously. You seem to know everything."

"I do not always know everything. Like you, I thought Browning was the murderer."

"It's a good thing you didn't tell DCI Williams that, he never would have let you hear the end of it if you'd gotten it wrong."

"That is why I do not tell him who my suspects are until I am completely certain. That, and what I told him was true: I have no faith that he will do his job well enough for a conviction, I must ensure that I have the criminal wrapped up for him and ready to deliver. But in this case, yes, I do know what has happened."

"Can you explain it to me?"

"There are two important points to remember in this story. The first one is that twice the blackmailing changed significantly. The first time was when the amount demanded went up significantly all at once. The second was when the letters stopped coming by hand and were instead delivered by e-mail. The second is especially significant because it occurred *after Elizabeth Dalton was murdered.* It means that she cannot be the sender of the e-mail."

The man came by to take our order. I ordered a sunshine smoothie, and Violet ordered a quinoa bowl of something-or-another that sounded exceedingly healthy and I was pretty sure had kale in it. When he left, Violet continued.

"The second important point to remember is that the bank account to pay the money into has changed. Yes, the bank is the same. But the account number is different. I believe that Elizabeth Dalton was discovered. Someone figured out what she was doing after around a month. This person, rather than telling Browning, told Dalton. They either asked, or threatened to be allowed in, and increased the payment amounts. That was when it went from being a few hundred pounds every few weeks to a thousand every two."

I nodded slowly as everything Violet was saying sunk in. It made perfect sense. "And so when Elizabeth Dalton was killed, this second, behind-the-scenes person decided to take over and continue blackmailing him."

"*Exactement.* That is the other reason why I believe it is this second person who is the true murderer now. If you had just learned that your partner in crime had been brutally murdered in the most painful way, and you assumed it was the person you had been blackmailing who was the guilty party, you would likely wait more than two days before you began to blackmail him once more, would you not?"

"Yes, a brutal death by strychnine is not one I would want to experience," I replied, shuddering slightly. There were some bad ways to go. Strychnine poisoning was definitely one of them.

"So now we're trying to find the person who was blackmailing Leo Browning, as they are the likely murderer. How on earth are we going to do that?" I asked. Violet shook her head slowly.

"I do not know yet. I need some time to think about it. But when I know what we will do, I will call you. I must stop after this at the police station, I want to give DCI Williams the bank account information of the second blackmailer. The second person is more experienced in that sort of thing. It is evidenced by the fact that they asked for more money. They used an untraceable e-mail account. Their bank account will be in the name of a business which will be untraceable as well. Of that, I am certain. But you never know, so it must be checked."

My smoothie and Violet's bowl arrived and we lunched in silence, each one of us caught up in our own thoughts. Who could have possibly figured out that Elizabeth Dalton was blackmailing Leo Browning? I had absolutely no idea.

CHAPTER 15

*A*n hour later I was back at my apartment, after having stopped at a shop I found on the way that sold more pet stuff. I got a few extra treats, and one of those toys with the little mouse on the end of a stick for Biscuit, as well as one of those tubes with the ball inside for him to play with also.

Of course, as soon as I unpacked them for him, Biscuit happily settled himself in the box and ignored the toys completely. Typical cat.

I played with Biscuit for a little bit, gave him a couple treats, then headed back out for a little bit to try and find a few decorations to make my new place my home. Two hours later I'd bought a framed photo of San Francisco that reminded me of home—it had been on sale for five pounds!—, some nice smelling candles, adorable animal-print tea towels for the kitchen, and a huge fleece blanket with a fox print on the front to curl up with. While I was in the mood to be productive and efficient, for once, I decided to go back to the hostel I'd been staying at and check out for good. I was well and truly a Londoner now, I thought to myself as I gave Biscuit a pat and promised him I'd take him out for a little bit when I got back.

I walked slowly back toward the hostel one last time. When I got there, I snuck my bike—the last possession of mine that I'd left in the room—back out the front door, then went back inside to hand in my keys. I couldn't help but be thankful to Violet. After all, if it wasn't for her, I'd probably still be spending my days mostly in bed, still deep in my depression. Violet gave me a reason to get up in the morning. She gave me something interesting to do. And I would always appreciate that.

Standing out in front of the hostel, knowing that I didn't live there anymore, my stomach began to grumble. I supposed it was getting to be around ten o'clock. The last thing I'd had to eat was that smoothie, and before that the McDonalds that was hours and hours ago.

Now that I actually had a place of my own, I was going to have to start cooking for myself more, I thought ruefully to myself, looking down at my waistline. But whatever, the diet could start tomorrow. Because after all, I no longer lived near a Chipotle restaurant; this might be my last chance to get a convenient, delicious burrito for a while.

A part of me recoiled at the thought. What if that

girl was working there again? What if she recognized me? What if she knew I was lying? No, I couldn't go there. It was off limits. Completely. But oh man, those burritos. In the end, my stomach won out. It being so late the streets were almost empty, so I rode my bicycle rather than walk it, letting the cool evening air blow onto my face as I made my way through the quaint London night.

The closer I got to Chipotle, the more I started wondering if this was a good idea. I was an anxiety-riddled mess, and all because I'd told a small lie a few days ago. Great. *Be an adult, and just go in there,* I thought to myself. *She probably isn't working, and if she is, she probably won't even recognize you anyway.*

Having given myself this little pep talk, I locked up my bike in front of the shop and went in. There she was, the same Australian redhead, working the counter. Great. On top of that, it was so late at night that while there were two people eating their food in a corner, I was the only person actually ordering.

I ordered my burrito, and the guy who made it slid it over to the girl.

"Hey, how's it going?" she asked in that same Australian accent.

"Good, you?" I replied.

"Yeah, I'm good, thanks. Big plans for tonight?"

I shrugged. "Not especially."

"Hey, you were here a few days ago, weren't you?"

My heart sunk. She knew. She knew I was lying.

"What? Oh, no, I don't think so," I said. I didn't

even know why I lied. I had no reason to lie. I could have just said yes. Why didn't I just say yes?

The color rose to my face and I began to panic. I looked around the room. The two people in the corner had their faces buried in their phones, and the guy who had made my burrito had gone into the back. I could just turn and run. I'd never be able to show my face here again, but at least I wouldn't have to explain myself. Running from my problems was a totally valid thing, right?

Of course, then I wouldn't get to eat my burrito.

"Hm, weird, I could have sworn you were in here a few days ago."

Finally, I broke down.

"I was! Oh my God, I'm so sorry, I was, and I don't know why I lied just then, but I have a weird friend who was telling me that I'm an awful liar and I should practice when it doesn't matter and you can't get caught in the lie and everything I told you that time too was a lie but I just can't do it anymore and I'm so sorry I didn't mean to and oh God what is wrong with me?"

Toward the end of that run-on sentence I could tell I was practically hysterical. Great. The girl at the counter was probably going to call the cops. Or a mental hospital. I wasn't sure which one was more appropriate. She stared at me for a minute, completely shocked, while I tried to do my best "I'm sorry, I'm not usually this insane" face. I wanted to apologize but I wasn't sure I trusted what was going to come out of my mouth. Suddenly, the girl did the complete opposite of what I expected: she burst out laughing.

"Oh thank God," I told her. "I thought you were about to call the cops on me. And you know, you would have totally been justified."

"You have a friend who told you to practice lying when it doesn't matter?" the Australian girl asked, still giggling. "By the way, you are the worst liar ever. Like, I had no idea you were lying, because quite frankly I barely cared about what you answered and was mostly just asking to pass the time. But at the slightest provocation you just broke completely. It was amazing. My cat is a better liar than you are."

This time it was my turn to laugh. "Well you don't have to rub it in. I can't believe I almost got away with it. You have no idea how close I came to not coming here tonight in case you remembered me and knew I lied the last time."

"On the bright side," the girl replied, "I know you don't work for the CIA. There's no way the Americans would have trusted you with state secrets."

"I kind of wish I'd kept up the lie. This is so embarrassing."

"Don't worry about it. Your friend sounds like a weirdo."

"Oh trust me, she is."

"I'm Brianne, by the way."

"Cassie," I replied.

"Is that your real name?" Brianne asked, arching an eyebrow.

"It is," I replied, giggling. "That time, I was telling the truth."

"So you don't actually work at... was it McDonalds?"

"No, I don't. I don't know why I said that. It was the first thing that came to my head."

"What do you do then?"

"I'm a doctor. Well, I'm not really a doctor." Brianne arched her eyebrow again. "No, no! I'm not actually lying to you," I said. "I was trained to be a doctor, but then I was in an accident, so I can't be a surgeon anymore. I kind of came to London to find myself, you know?"

Brianne nodded. "I can understand that. If I asked you what a septal myectomy was, what would you tell me?"

"Are you testing me?" I asked.

"Can you blame me?" Brianne replied with a wink.

"It's open heart surgery that removes thickened septum from the heart to improve blood flow," I replied, sticking my tongue out at her. "How do you know what that is, anyway?"

"There's a lot to learn at a minimum wage job at Chipotle that you wouldn't expect," she joked. "But seriously, I'm actually taking medicine at uni myself right now. I'm at Barts and the London. This job just pays my rent."

"Well, if you ever need a hand—a metaphorical one anyway—I know a lot of stuff that I can't put to use anymore," I told her, holding up my slightly deformed left hand.

"I'm sorry," Brianne replied, her face filling with sympathy. "It must be tough, having done all that training, and then not being able to practice."

"It is. I left America because I was just too depressed, moping around all the time." I didn't know why I was telling Brianne all this. She just seemed nice, and understanding.

"Well, listen, what's your number? Let me send you a text. We should hang out sometime, grab a drink or something."

"Sure," I replied, smiling. "That sounds fun."

I would have never guessed that I'd have walked into the Mexican restaurant looking for a burrito, and come out of it with a new friend.

CHAPTER 16

I took my burrito back home and ate it at the kitchen counter, while Biscuit tried his best to sneak his way into stealing it from me as well. We were going to have to set some boundaries for the mischievous little guy. It was almost eleven by the time I got back, but I put him in his harness and took him outside for a little bit, letting him explore his new neighborhood. This was a good time; it was late enough that there was no one on the street to see me walking a cat on a leash. Luckily for Biscuit, my desire to see him happily wandering around was greater than my own shame. After all, I'd embarrassed myself so much tonight that surely compared to being caught lying to Brianne, walking a cat on a leash wasn't too bad.

When we got back in I lay down on the couch and decided to watch a bit of TV. I was, however, quite a bit more tired than I expected, and quickly found myself completely passed out.

I woke up the next day to one of those cute little historical English mysteries on TV. Biscuit was curled up in the nook of my arm against the couch, which obviously meant I couldn't move, or I'd wake him up. So instead, I decided to watch some of the TV show. Apparently there was a killer going around in a little village up in northern England somewhere, and it seemed he'd already killed three people, all tall, brunette women.

The policeman in charge had no idea what to do. Funnily enough, he reminded me a little bit of DCI Williams. Maybe it was the red hair. Anyway, he decided he was going to use the one piece of information he definitely had: knowledge of the killers' targets, and set a trap. He got a tall, brunette police-woman to wander around town at the same time as the killer was known to strike, and followed her closely. When the man came up to her and tried to kidnap her, the policeman jumped in and saved the day.

As the end credits rolled, I jumped up excitedly. Biscuit, falling to the floor—but still landing on his feet of course—let out a loud meow of discontent.

"Sorry Biscuit," I apologized, running to the counter where I'd left my phone. "I didn't mean to, but I have to text Violet. I think I may have figured out how to catch a killer!"

* * *

FIVE MINUTES later I was knocking on Violet's front door. She'd said to come by immediately, so I threw on some clothes, ran a brush through my hair, left some breakfast out for Biscuit—along with a treat as an apology—and headed over. She led me into the study, the same room as I'd been in the last time. I sat on the couch as Violet perched herself on the edge of the desk.

"So? What is it that you have thought of?" she asked.

"Well, see I was watching one of those detective shows on TV just now. And the policeman only had one thing to go by: the preferred hair color and size of the women he was targeting. So he set a trap based on that."

"And so you propose that we set a trap as well?"

"Yes! After all, we have the bank account details of the person who is still blackmailing Leo Browning, and who likely killed Elizabeth Dalton. What if we somehow lured them to the bank? Like, if we told them there was a problem with their account, or something?"

Violet nodded slowly. "Yes. Yes, I could see how that could work. As it is Saturday there is nothing to be done right now. I will organize this over the weekend, and on Monday, we will catch ourselves a murderer."

About three hours later, I decided I was going to

be an adult, and that included grocery shopping. After all, as much as I enjoyed subsisting entirely on take-out food, I was pretty sure my waistline wasn't going to enjoy it that much. I spent the morning enjoying Biscuit's company and watching the news on TV, then I got changed and headed out.

As I walked past Violet's place, however, I ran into someone with mussed-up blonde hair, twinkling blue eyes and a smile to die for. He was wearing slacks and a polo shirt today; tight clothes that showed off just how much time he must spend in the gym. Jake Edmonds, also known as Doctor Gorgeous, was on my street. And he started talking to me.

"Cassie, hi!" he said as he came toward me. Oh my God. I was dressed for a mid-day run to the local grocery store, wearing an oversized cat-print sweater and leggings. I was so not dressed for a random meeting with the hottest guy in London. I silently thanked God that I'd at least thought to brush my hair and tie it up in a ponytail. That was something, right?

"Oh, Jake, hey," I said, trying to flash a sexy smile that felt more like a grimace. Ugh. I was so out of practice at flirting. The last time I had a boyfriend had to have been at least eighteen months ago, probably closer to two years. "What are you doing here?"

I winced as soon as I said the words. They sounded so accusatory. Great. Grill the hot guy about why he's on your street, great idea, Cassie, I thought to myself.

"I'm dropping off a copy of an autopsy for Violet. Don't worry, it's not the case you're working on. She wanted it as soon as possible."

"She doesn't really seem like the patient type," I replied, and Jake laughed.

"That's true. So what are your plans for the day?"

"Well, I was just going to run out and get groceries, then I was thinking I might do the tourist thing for a while. You know, get to know London and stuff?"

That second part wasn't exactly true, in the sense that I hadn't really planned on doing it, but it wasn't totally a lie, either. I had looked at Google maps the other day and seen that I now lived only a few blocks away from the Natural History Museum, the Science Museum and the Victoria and Albert Museum, and had thought to myself that I should definitely give them a visit.

"Hey, if you want a quintessential London experience, why don't you come join me at the Queen's Arms? Every time I leave Violet's place I feel like drinking heavily, and there's a great pub nearby."

I was pretty sure I just stopped and stared at Jake without saying anything for at least a full minute.

"Yeah, sure," I finally stammered out, and he grinned.

"Awesome. As fun as it is to sit at a bar drinking alone, it's always better with someone else," he joked.

I laughed a little bit too hard and tried to calm down the multitude of feelings happening inside of me. This wasn't a date, I reminded myself. This was a guy who just wanted someone to chat to while he drank a beer. So not a date.

"I can see how Violet can drive people to drink," I said as we headed back down the street.

"She is pretty intense. But she's extremely good at what she does. Honestly, I'd rather have a police force made up entirely of people like her."

"So you agree with her then, that all cops are idiots?"

"Well, I don't go that far. But let's just say a few of the police stations have a few people who have risen up the ranks a tad further than their intelligence should have allowed them to."

I laughed. "I know what you mean. There were a few of those in medical school as well. Luckily they were all weeded out before they actually got to practice."

We walked up a lane that was so quintessentially English, I couldn't help but stare around. Old brick buildings rose up on either side of us, about three stories tall. Gorgeous, colorful flowers bloomed out the front, lushly leaved trees rose up at steady intervals, and some of the walls were even covered in ivy!

At the end of the road, on the corner, was a fairly nondescript building whose ground floor was painted in teal, with flower pots hanging from the walls. Two old school blackboards out the front advertised the specials.

"This is the place," Jake said, leading me inside.

The dark hardwood floor creaked underfoot as we stepped inside. The place had a dark, classically British ambiance. To one side was a dark wooden bar, glasses and bottles of spirits piled high on the shelves behind. Jake and I sat at a table in a corner by the window, looking out to the road, on a couple of dark stools. Dim lighting set the mood as city workers and locals alike crowded together, drinking glasses of beer and eating delicious looking food.

"What can I get you to drink?" Jake asked. I wasn't normally much of a beer drinker, but the ambiance here seemed to demand it.

"Whatever beer's good," I said, and he came back with a glass of ale with a nice head on it. I sipped it carefully, half expecting the beer to be room temperature, having heard all the jokes about how that was the way the English liked their beer. Luckily for me, it seemed that was one stereotype that wasn't actually true, as the beer was nicely chilled, and tasted pretty good.

For a minute we just sat there sipping our beer. I was honestly a bit afraid to ask Jake anything. I was so out of practice at flirting that I was pretty sure if I tried to ask him anything I'd probably get flustered, fall off my stool and knock my beer all over myself on my way down.

"So what part of America are you from?" Jake asked. Good, this was an easy question. I could probably answer this without falling all over myself in an attempt to impress the hottest guy ever.

"San Francisco," I said. "I'm a California girl through and through, despite the lack of blonde hair."

"Really? You gave up year-round sunshine and the ocean for the London weather that can only be kindly described as 'woefully depressing'?"

I laughed. "I just needed a change. Something completely different. Plus, my dad was born in Scotland, so I have a UK passport. It makes it easier than going through all that visa stuff to live somewhere else."

"So you've moved here for good then?"

"I'm not sure," I replied. "I'm not really good with long-term plans. This move was more of an on-a-whim sort of thing. How about you, how long have you worked at the coroner's office?"

"About two years. I worked at a hospital for a couple of years after finishing my studies, then moved into the coroner's office."

"What made you go into pathology?"

"I discovered pretty quickly when I started medical school that I hated most patients."

I burst out laughing. "That's half the reason I went into surgery," I replied. "All the important stuff is done when they're asleep and they can't complain about what you're doing."

"I know, right? My first year I was following a doctor doing his rounds, and there was a lady there that refused to tell him any of her symptoms because of 'privacy reasons'. He asked her how she expected him to diagnose her, and she told him that if he was a good enough doctor he should be able to figure it out, since after all, that's what vets do all day."

I burst out laughing. "No way! What did the doctor say to that?"

"He told her if she wanted to be as stubborn as a bull there was a veterinary clinic just up the road."

"Wow!" I laughed. "That's amazing. Did he get in trouble for it?"

Jake grinned. "Well the woman complained, and I think the doctor got a half-arsed dressing down from the hospital director, but that was it."

"Oh man, that's crazy. I once got to watch a knee surgery, a meniscus repair, where the patient remained awake the whole time. He spent the entire surgery asking the doctor to explain in detail what he was doing and why. Eventually the doctor said if the guy didn't let him do his job he was going to have to put him under completely."

"People are nuts," Jake said, shaking his head. "Of course, not working with patients—live ones anyway—means you don't see the crazy things people come in with to Accident and Emergency."

"First thing you learn in medical school," I replied. "There's nothing people won't stick in their rectums."

"The worst I saw was a half-full container of raspberry jam."

"Well, I'm glad you can still be an optimist after seeing that," I joked, earning myself a hearty laugh from Jake. I liked his laugh. It was sincere, and it lit up his face and made him look even better than he normally did.

"So do you work at a hospital in London yet? Or has Violet hired you to be her own personal doctor, since she apparently doesn't trust us?" Jake asked.

I laughed. "Don't take it personally."

"Oh, I never take anything Violet does personally. I don't think she realizes she's the way she is half the time."

"Agreed. But in this particular case, she didn't hire me at all." I explained to Jake how we'd met in the police station when I went to the wrong floor, and how she invited me to tag along on her cases.

"Oh, so she was telling the truth when she said she was showing you around London."

"She certainly was. In fact, for all the teasing we do about how socially inept she is, I think she's a lot more perceptive about people than she lets on."

"That wouldn't surprise me at all. Violet is very good at acting."

My face began to flush red at the memory of that incredibly awkward moment she'd created inside the morgue. *Don't mention it. Don't mention it. Don't mention it.*

"She could have done without that comment the other day in the morgue."

What was wrong with me? It was like something in my brain was wired to completely ruin everything whenever I was in front of this incredibly friendly, funny, super-hot guy that I was now sharing a beer with. Could I possibly be worse at flirting? Thankfully, Jake just laughed.

"Yeah, that was classic Violet. Trust me, she's worse when you're actually *in* a relationship. You can't hide it from her. She just knows."

I laughed. "That sounds about right. I'm still not totally sure she's completely human."

"Definitely. So you say you're a surgeon?"

"Well… not anymore. I was trained to be a surgeon." Maybe it was the beer. Maybe it was the fact that Jake seemed like he'd understand. I told him everything. From the night I got hit by a car, to the moment I hit rock bottom, to when I decided to move to England on a whim, in a last-ditch attempt to get myself out of my depression.

"Damn," Jake said softly when I was finished. "You need this beer more than I do."

I couldn't help myself, I laughed.

"Seriously though," he continued. "I'm really sorry. What you went through, that's incredibly tough. I think what you're doing is good. Don't rush into any decisions. You have lots of time to think things through. But let me tell you: there is hope. There are lots of specialties that aren't surgery but also aren't doing general practice for the rest of your life. You might find something you love. And if not, well, you'll find something you like to do in another career path. But it's all right to be depressed. Everything you're feeling is normal. There's nothing wrong with you."

I smiled at him. "Thanks," I said. Funnily enough, that was the first time anyone had actually treated me like I was a normal person when I mentioned my depression.

"So that's what you meant when you said Violet was perceptive."

I nodded. "Yeah. I think she could tell, you know? That I needed something to do."

"Well, take it as a compliment. I've never known Violet to willingly hang around anyone, so it's more than just that. I'm at least ninety percent sure that if I called her tonight and told her I was thinking of committing suicide she'd just tell me there were hotlines for that and hang up."

I laughed. "She does give off a bit of a vibe that you never really know what's coming, doesn't she?"

Jake and I kept chatting. I found out he lived in a small flat in Mayfair, alone. He was the only child of two doctors, and had been chosen from birth to follow in his parents' footsteps. Luckily for everybody involved, Jake loved medicine, and he had never resented them for pushing him in that direction.

I told him about life in San Francisco, and he told me about growing up in London. Before I knew it, the sky outside began to darken, and we realized we'd been sitting there talking for hours.

"I should probably go back home," I said finally.

"Yeah, me too."

Neither one of us really made a move to go, though. Eventually, however, we made our way back outside. Shoot. What do I do now? This wasn't a date, we'd just talked. But it still felt fairly intimate.

"So, uh, see you around, I guess," I finally said. Jake grinned.

"I swear, sometimes you act like you're in year eight trying to figure out how to talk to boys," he told me. "What's your phone number? I'd like to take you out to dinner one night."

I tried to hide the fact that my insides were essentially jumping around with glee. I grabbed my phone out of my purse so eagerly that I immediately dropped it on the ground and swore as I picked it up.

"Sorry," I said, realizing that wasn't exactly lady-like. Jake just laughed.

I got his number off him and sent him a text. This was happening! Doctor Gorgeous wanted my phone number! Ahh!

"Cool. I'll walk you home, then head down to the tube station from there," he told me. I tried not to skip along like a five-year-old the whole way, I was so excited. In fact, I was way too excited for a thirty-year-old woman to be going on a first date. But with a man like Jake? Yes, please! I was half tempted to invite him straight into my apartment, but then I thought that might be a bit too forward. I didn't want him to think I was that easy. And I wasn't. Unless the guy looked like *him*.

We walked more or less in silence, with me silently wishing he'd take my arm in his or something, and we could stroll through the quaint streets of London like an old-timey couple. My daydream was over almost as soon as it began and we found ourselves at my front door.

"All right, I'll see you around," Jake said with a wink, and he turned around and left. I liked to imagine it was because he didn't trust himself so close to my bedroom.

Heading back inside, my heart giddy with excitement, the last thing on my mind was the forgotten groceries. "I have a potential boyfriend!" I announced to Biscuit, picking him up by the armpits and swinging him around the room. Biscuit was not nearly as enthusiastic about this as I was, and he gave me a dirty look when I put him back down.

I was so happy I gave him a little treat as an apology. I hadn't been this happy in a long time. Maybe things were finally turning around for me.

CHAPTER 17

*A*fter an uneventful Sunday, in which I simply spent the day lying around watching TV and playing with Biscuit—after the crazy week with Violet I figured I'd earned it—I woke up Monday morning to a text from Violet.

Be ready to go in fifteen minutes.

I supposed I shouldn't have been that upset. After all, she didn't send me the text until just after nine in the morning, when normal people were already awake. But I'd had a long day of doing nothing, and so I'd slept in. I was *so* going to need longer than fifteen minutes. I rushed to get ready, and just managed to finish putting my hair up into a ponytail as Violet knocked at my door. I grabbed my purse and rushed out, giving Biscuit a quick pat and a promise to be back later on my way out.

"How was your date with Doctor Edmonds?" she

asked me as we walked down to the main street and hailed a cab.

"How could you *possibly* know about that?" I asked. "Besides, it wasn't a date."

"Maybe not, but you were gone for four hours."

"Do you just spend the whole day sitting at your window and spying on the street like an old gossip with nothing better to do?"

Violet smiled. "No. In fact, I did not know how long you had gone out for. I saw the two of you leave together, but then I went and worked on the case for which Doctor Edmonds had brought me the files. I simply threw out a number, and I knew if I had been wrong, you would have corrected me."

I groaned. It was way too early in the morning to deal with Violet. Luckily, she quickly moved on to the events of the day.

"The idea that you told me this weekend, it was not a bad one. I think we found a way to make it work."

"So everything is all set?" I asked.

"Yes. I have a friend at the bank who owes me a favor. We have worked with him, and with Leonard Browning." On the way there, Violet explained to me the rest of the plan.

"Browning is supposed to deposit another one thousand pounds into the bank account today. What will happen is he will leave the office for a while, go to the bank, go back to the office, and send an email to the person saying that the transaction was unable to be completed, and that they have to contact the bank to sort it out. My person at the bank will ensure that anyone calling about that specific account will be put through to him. He will tell the blackmailer that there was an issue with the tax information supplied with the account, and that they have to put a hold on the account until the proper documents are brought in and put on file."

"How will we know who the blackmailer is?" I asked. "After all, there have to be hundreds of people that work at those offices."

Violet took her phone out and handed it to me. She'd opened Safari to the *Meet Our Team* section of the Enderby Insurance website. I scrolled through the corporate headshots of dozens of people, nodding slowly.

"I memorized these yesterday. Do not worry. When someone comes in, we will know."

"What about the police? Have you called them?"

"And immediately scare away our killer? No, I have not called the police."

"But they can come in plain clothes," I offered, and Violet laughed.

"A policeman in plain clothes is similar to two children standing on each other's shoulders wearing a long coat in an attempt to view an adult only movie. They may at a glance look legitimate, but it very quickly becomes obvious who they really are. Do not worry. It will be fine."

Violet seemed so sure of herself that I let the

matter drop. After all, I reminded myself, this was not the first time she had done something like this. Catching criminals on her own was what Violet did. She'd probably gone through something like this hundreds of times.

The cab dropped us off in front of the London Haymarket branch of Virgin Money.

"This is the main London branch," Violet explained. "My contact works here. He will tell whoever the blackmailer is to come here."

From the outside, the bank looked pretty small and unassuming. As soon as we stepped inside, however, it was like a completely different world. For one thing, everything was so *colorful!* To the left, a large red barrier led downstairs to a lounge area. Straight ahead were the banking facilities, complete with booths where transactions could be completed with iPads, as well as bank employees willing to help customers. Violet led me slightly to the right, where bright red, deep purple and sky blue couches, chairs and booths lined the walls, huge ball-shaped lights overhead brightening up the space. The walls were red on one side, purple on the other. The whole thing gave a bit of an impression of being a giant play-ground more than a bank.

We sat down in one of the little booths on the side. Violet faced the door directly; I sat next to her so with a glance to my left I could see anyone who was coming as well. In front of us, a giant TV screen advertised the products and services available at Virgin Money.

Violet's phone buzzed to indicate a text, and she read it and nodded.

"The blackmailer has called the bank. She will be arriving shortly. That is right, I have been told that the person on the phone was a woman. That narrows our search considerably."

It took everything in my power not to just wrench my head to the side and stare at the entrance to the bank. After all, we had to be subtle about this. The last thing I wanted to do was to spook away our murderer. I scrolled through the list of people who worked at Enderby Insurance on my own phone, and found that every single time anyone with the slightest resemblance to anyone on the list entered the bank, my heart skipped a beat. I kept having to remind myself that there were millions of people in London, and only one person from this list was supposed to be in this bank this morning. I had to be patient. After all, it might take the person a little while to collect the information they needed to bring in, as well. We could be here for hours, I told myself.

But, as it turned out, it wasn't nearly that long. Just a little more than forty minutes after Violet got the text, a short haired brunette walked in that not only looked like one of the headshots on the website, but looked familiar to me. I'd met her! It was Jennifer Ashton.

I couldn't help myself. I sat there and stared with my mouth dropped open. Her? Really?

Violet put on an overly cheerful smile and waved as Jennifer looked around. She looked hurried, frantic and nervous. Like she didn't want to be here. She saw Violet, and for a moment I could have sworn her face fell completely. But, she quickly plastered on a smile and efficiently came over to see us.

"Miss Despuis, Ms. Coburn," she said, nodding to each of us. "What an unlikely coincidence. I do hope you're doing well, but if you'll excuse me, I have a very important appointment here at the bank."

"Ah, but Ms. Ashton, you are in exactly the right place. After all, your appointment is here, with the two of us," Violet said, motioning for Jennifer Ashton to sit down at the seat across from us. Jennifer looked at us both askance, untrusting.

"No, I have a real appointment, with Mr. Fredericks," she replied, but Violet shook her head.

"That was my doing, I apologize. But you see, there was no other way to know who truly owned the bank account to which Leonard Browning was supposed to send the money. I received word from my contact in the police department last night. You were intelligent to register a company in Ireland, where shell company providers ask for little to no identification. So alas, you left me no choice but to set this trap."

Jennifer Ashton's face went paler and paler the more Violet spoke.

"Please, Miss Ashton, sit. You do not look well," Violet implored once more. "These seats are far more comfortable than those at the police station, and I must humbly say that I am a much better listener than the brutes at the Metropolitan Police."

This time, Jennifer sat down across from us. It was a good thing, too. I was fairly confident that if she'd tried to stay upright she'd have simply fallen over.

Her face was pale, but she remained as stoic as ever. Her lips were pressed firmly together. "I have no idea what you're talking about," she finally said.

"I'm not quite certain if you are playing stupid, or if you simply *are* stupid," Violet said in response. Wow. I had to keep that scorcher in my pocket for a later date. "But you know who I am, yes?"

Jennifer Ashton nodded. Apparently she no longer trusted herself to actually speak. Violet leaned forward and continued. "So you know that I have stopped hundreds of criminals. I am wondering what makes you possibly think you would be more intelligent than them?"

It took almost a full minute before Jennifer replied. "I… I don't," she finally stammered. "I simply have… I have no idea what you're talking about."

"Ah!" Violet said. "But you insult my intelligence. And I must tell you, up until now, I had been quite impressed with yours. It takes a certain finesse to murder someone entirely unrelated to your eventual target."

I didn't think it was possible, but Jennifer Ashton's face had gone even paler.

"Fine," she admitted. "I was blackmailing Leonard Browning. But that's all. I didn't kill Elizabeth Dalton. I barely even knew her."

"You do not need to know someone to go into business with them. Especially when that business is an unsavoury type. You say you did not know Elizabeth Dalton. Let me tell you a little bit about her." Violet leaned back in the chair and closed her eyes. How could she possibly be so relaxed, knowing there was a murderer sitting right in front of us? She quickly began talking. "Elizabeth Dalton was the motherly type. She had no children of her own, so she took to caring for the young girls in the office. She was not a rich woman, by any means. In fact, she had debts. And Elizabeth Dalton, I must say, *was not a happy woman.* She was approaching her retirement years. She had no children. No husband. No money. And no happiness. I imagine she walked through London and saw the beautiful women with their expensive bags, their nice shoes, and she wanted that to be her. But she had no way to do it."

Violet's eyes opened suddenly. Jennifer Ashton was fixated on Violet, as though if she stared hard enough Violet might spontaneously combust. I had to admit, Violet had a riveting way of speaking, and I was fairly fixed on the story as well, even though I knew all the same facts.

"Until the scandal with Edgar Enderby," Violet said so quietly it was almost a whisper.

"How do you know about that? No one outside the firm was supposed to know about that," Jennifer Ashton said. Violet only smiled in reply before continuing her narrative.

"Elizabeth Dalton got a good lesson in how the world worked: if you had information on someone, you could use it to your advantage. Edgar Enderby had been kicked out of the firm completely. Him! The son of the president, over the lowly secretary! Unbelievable. Elizabeth Dalton had never truly expected her plan with the video to work. She simply wanted to show an example for the girls in the office, that when there is a bully, you stand up to them, like a good motherly figure would. But her plan did work! And slowly, a plan began to form in Elizabeth Dalton's head. A plan to allow her to be like the other women she saw. Like the powerful women, the ones with money. Being the motherly type, Elizabeth was privy to much of the gossip that occurred between the young girls. For instance, it was rumoured that Chelsea Flannigan was having an affair with none other than Elizabeth's boss, Leonard Browning. And for someone in Elizabeth's position, it would not have been the least bit difficult to find proof of the affair, knowing that it was happening. So she found it. But Elizabeth Dalton was not a sophisticated woman. No, she was not like the confident, strong businesswomen she aspired to be. So her methods were crude. She asked for a simple two hundred pounds per fortnight. A fortune to her, a drop in the bucket to Browning. But to her credit, she did not flaunt her new money. She continued to take her old raggedy purses to work, and wear her comfortable shoes. In all of the photos of her in the newsletter she wears what she always wore, there is not a designer bag in sight. She did not want Browning to realize it was her who was blackmailing him. In a way, she was cleverer than she acted."

Violet leaned forward toward Jennifer and smiled. Her eyes were twinkling. She was enjoying this. "But you! No, you were exactly what Elizabeth Dalton wanted to be. You knew that Leonard Browning could afford far more than two hundred pounds a fortnight. You discovered that she was blackmailing him. But rather than expose her, you joined her."

Jennifer Ashton made a sound in her throat that sounded a little bit like a cat coughing up a hairball. "Yes, soon Mr. Browning found he was having to pay one thousand pounds per fortnight. But I have a feeling it wasn't about the money for you, was it?"

Jennifer looked like she wanted to puke. Violet waited patiently for the reply. When Jennifer finally answered, it was with an anger and a vitriol I didn't know she could muster.

"That's right. I wanted that tosser to quit. He only got that job because of the old boys' club. I had been at the company longer. I was better at my job. But because of my genitals, I was passed over. I ran into

Elizabeth Dalton in the wine shop by our work one weekend when I had some extra work to do. She was all decked out, carrying a Prada handbag. I almost couldn't believe it was her! I had no idea where she'd gotten the money from, but I quickly pieced together the puzzle. I went to see her, and I explained to her that we could do better. And we did! We were doing well. I could tell the pressure was getting to him. I had planned to make it more difficult, to demand fifteen hundred a fortnight. He was going to have to leave before we bankrupted him."

"And that was where you fell into difficulties." Jennifer Ashton nodded. It was like now, once she started talking, she couldn't stop.

"Yes. Elizabeth didn't want to go overboard. She just wanted a little bit of money to play with. She told me this was going too far. That she couldn't go further. She was happy to continue blackmailing Browning, but only at the current rate."

"*Eh bien*, that was when you realized that if you wanted Browning out of the office for good, you were going to have to be even cleverer."

"What? No, as I said, I didn't murder Elizabeth Dalton."

"Ah, but you did," Violet said. Violet's eyes bored into Jennifer Ashton once more. "You knew that Elizabeth Dalton ate lunch at that soup stall every day. You put the poison into the soup, expecting that many people would die. You thought the police would see a serial killer, not a targeted murder."

Jennifer Ashton's lips parted as her face took on an expression of horror. "And you see, you were correct. The police looked for a serial killer. But you forgot about one thing. *Moi!* You did not expect me to take the case. You did not expect me to immediately discover that the murders were not the work of a random lunatic. But you were not stupid. You did not kill Browning with poison in case it was discovered that it was not random. Because then, you would be a suspect. You attempted to frame Leonard Browning as your backup plan. After all, you could not simply murder him. You had much too strong a motive. The spurned underling, the career woman looking to make a name for herself. No, you could not attract so much attention to yourself."

Violet paused for a minute, and then continued.

"You killed Elizabeth Dalton in the hopes that, if it were discovered that she was the target, that Browning would be found to be the killer. However, you did not know that he was called away to Manchester on business that day at the last minute. You did not know until later that it was impossible for him to have committed the crime. As soon as you discovered that your plan had failed, you went back to blackmailing him, only this time you doubled the amount, hoping to put so much pressure on him that he would find another position elsewhere. He would leave the company, no matter what, leaving his position open to his second-in-command."

"You have no evidence of this. None whatsoever,"

Jennifer Ashton finally said. Her voice was filled with fear. I was honestly amazed. We were sitting here, just inches away from a woman who had killed four people in an attempt to take her boss' job, and *she* was the one who was scared.

"You are correct. I do not. However, you know of me. You have seen how easily I have uncovered the exact operation. Do you truly believe it will take me long to find enough evidence against you to convict you in court?"

Jennifer sighed. "No. No, of course I do not. Do you mind if we step outside for a moment? After all, I am free to go. I see no policemen here."

"That is correct. There are no policemen here. However, I encourage you to turn yourself in. If you admit to your crimes before I am able to prove them beyond a doubt, I am certain that you will be given leniency. For now, we go outside. You do look as though you could use some air."

CHAPTER 18

I looked curiously at Violet as the three of us got up. What exactly had been the plan here? Violet had shown her hand completely, Jennifer had denied everything, and now she was getting ready to leave. Surely there was a plan here I didn't know about, because right now it seemed like everything was going badly. This wasn't like in the movies or on TV, when the guilty party was confronted and admitted to everything. What on earth were we going to do?

Violet led the way outside with Jennifer Ashton following behind her, trying in vain to maintain a confident air of authority. I took up the rear. Violet led us to the small alleyway next to the bank. Even though we were only a few feet away from the hustle and bustle of downtown London, the alley somehow muted the sounds of the city. People walked past, completely oblivious to our presence just a few feet away. I had a bad feeling about this, and glanced out to the street.

Jennifer Ashton leaned against the wall, taking deep breaths. She was obviously trying to find her way out of this.

"You may as well turn yourself in," Violet told her. "I will find the proof. It will not take me long."

Jennifer's eyes flashed in anger. "No," she said. "I will not. Like every arrogant person on the planet, you wouldn't have told the police about this, would you?"

"No, not yet," Violet replied calmly. Jennifer dug through her purse. Suddenly, she pulled out a Swiss Army knife. My eyes widened as she flipped open the blade, and I shrunk back against the wall, but Violet just smiled. It was as though she'd expected this the whole time.

"That's the problem with you arrogant types. You always keep everything to yourselves. I worked too hard to get here. I'm not going to let you ruin this for me."

My throat was dry. Every instinct in my body was telling me to run, but I also knew it was pointless. Ever since my surgery, not only was I in terrible shape, but my left leg didn't work quite as well as it should; there were small children who could run faster than me now.

Jennifer looked over at me. It was like she could tell I was the weaker target. Clutching the knife, she looked stronger now. She had the upper hand on us, and she knew it. The knife wasn't big, but I was all too aware of just how much damage it could do. I'd seen people in the ICU, hell, I'd seen people in the morgue thanks to wounds the same size as that knife she wielded.

Kicking off her heels, Jennifer lunged at me. I cowered back against the far wall. My body froze. There was nothing I could do except look at the steel blade as it came closer and closer to me. My breath caught in my throat. I couldn't fight or flight. I was stuck. Frozen to the spot, and like a deer caught in headlights, I was about to be killed.

No. No, I wouldn't be killed. Or if I was, I was going to fight back. It wasn't going to be like this. I was going to give it everything. I had too much to live for. I didn't want to die.

At the last second I darted to the left as Jennifer reached out to slash me with the knife. She grunted in disapproval and lunged at me again, but this time I managed to move back and out of the way. She ran toward me again, but this time, she kicked out at me. Making contact with my bad knee, I cried out and fell to the ground, clutching at my knee in pain. This time, there was nothing for me to do. Nowhere for me to go. I couldn't do anything with my knee hurting like this. Jennifer lunged forward once more as a tear began to fall down my cheek. I didn't want to die.

I closed my eyes, silently told my mom I loved her, but there was no pain. Nothing. I cautiously opened my eyes and found Violet in front of me. Her shoulder was bleeding, oozing blood onto her shirt, but she was holding the hand with Jennifer's knife. With a single quick movement, she kicked out and swiped Jennifer's legs from underneath her. The woman fell to the ground with a yelp, and with a single quick movement Violet flipped her onto her stomach, forcing her arm behind her and twisting until Jennifer dropped the blade.

Coming to my senses, I ran forward and grabbed it while Violet kept her knee firmly in Jennifer's back. She grabbed the woman's hair, pulled up her head and drove it into the pavement. Jennifer Ashton stopped moving; she was knocked unconscious. Violet then calmly took out her phone and dialled a number. I assumed it was an ambulance.

"Hello, DCI Williams. Yes, if you come to the Virgin Money branch at Haymarket I have a gift for you. A gift that you can charge with four counts of murder and two counts of attempted murder."

There was a pause. "Of course we're all right, I did say *attempted*, didn't I? Or was that too long a word for you?"

I smiled to myself, then the instincts that came from twelve years of schooling kicked into gear. Violet was bleeding from her shoulder; I had to take care of that.

I grabbed my phone and started dialling nine-one-one, before remembering the number here was different. I stopped the call and began to press nine-nine-nine instead, but Violet stopped me.

"Goodness, Cassie, you're acting like I'm going to die."

"You might, if you don't get medical attention soon," I replied.

"If only I knew a doctor. Hmm, it's too bad there's not one standing right here," Violet replied. I dialed the number and put the phone on speaker, then went over to look at the wound.

"Yes, we need an ambulance at uh, the corner of Haymarket and Shaver's Place," I said, looking up for the street sign indicating the name of the lane we were standing in. Carefully, I had a look at the wound in Cassie's shoulder. It was oozing blood, dark blood. That meant it was a vein that had been hit, not an artery. That was good. That was very good. There was a decent amount of blood, but not an amount that would be life-threatening if I applied pressure to the wound.

Jennifer Ashton's purse had a scarf attached to the side of it, to make it look fancier. I ran over and grabbed it, then bunched up the scarf and pressed it against Violet's wound.

"As useful as it is to have a doctor around, I can't just magically create antibiotics out of mid-air," I told Violet as I worked to stop the bleeding. It wasn't so bad that she was going to need a tourniquet. Plus, the ambulance would be here in a few minutes, so just applying pressure with the scarf should be fine for now.

"I do not need an ambulance," Violet repeated. "I am fine."

"Really? Because you were just stabbed while saving my life. And besides, I'm a doctor. You have to listen to me. If I say you need an ambulance, you need an ambulance."

I made sure Jennifer Ashton was well and truly unconscious—and checked her pulse just in case, she was still very much alive—and led Violet over to the wall, where I sat her down.

"Don't lie down, I want your shoulder to stay above your heart," I ordered. "Keep the bandage pressed against the wound."

I was about to go out to the street to see if the ambulance was arriving yet, when DCI Williams suddenly turned the corner. I waved over to him, and he rushed over.

"Violet! What happened? Are you all right?" he asked, concern etched all over his face.

"I am. I have your murderer. She's lying over there," Violet said, motioning with her head toward Jennifer Ashton.

"It's all right," I told him. "I called the ambulance, they're on their way."

"Good, well done Miss Coburn," DCI Williams replied with a nod as he made his way to Jennifer Ashton. She was just beginning to stir back to life, and he cuffed her before she was able to do anything else.

"I'll come by and get your statement later from the hospital," he called out to Violet and I as he led her away.

"We won't be at the hospital, I'm fine," Violet called back toward him. I had to fight the urge to roll my eyes.

"Really? You're fine? Because you've just been stabbed in the shoulder. That's not 'fine'," I scolded.

Violet shrugged, wincing slightly at the pain as she moved her shoulder. "It's not like it's the first time."

"Oh, so you make it a habit to be attacked by murderers?"

"You should be a little bit more grateful. After all, I did save your life."

"Yes, you did, and I am thankful, but as a doctor I also have to do my best to save yours. As much as I'm tempted to let you bleed to death in this alley right now just to show you that you *do* need medical attention."

"I am fine. A bit of pressure on the wound, a few stitches, and everything will be all right. I've been here before. I am not a baby; I know what it is like to be stabbed."

Violet was impossible. I shook my head in disbelief as the ambulance pulled up. I directed them toward Violet.

"No matter what, insist she goes to the hospital," I said to one of them quietly.

"I heard that," Violet called out to me.

"Doctor's orders," I called back.

"You're not licensed to practice in this country!" she called back.

"Somehow I don't think that's the sort of thing you usually care about," I replied. The paramedics quickly huddled themselves around Violet and loaded her up onto a stretcher, despite her protestations. I hopped into the ambulance along with them, Violet eventually giving up and lying down on the stretcher while the EMTs inserted an IV, cut off her shirt and worked to clean the wound and stop the bleeding.

Half an hour later we were in the hospital, Violet lying in a bed in the ICU. She was quiet now, she'd resigned herself to her fate of receiving necessary medical attention.

"Thanks for saving my life," I said to her quietly as she lay on the bed.

"Do not mention it. How is your knee?"

"A little bit sore. I'll go see a physiotherapist if it's not better in a few days, but I think it was simply the shock of it."

Violet nodded. "Good."

"Did you know?" I asked. "That she was going to attack us?"

"I had a pretty good idea."

"Then why do it at all? That was so dangerous."

"Because it was the fastest way to get her arrested. Even if she does not admit to the murders now, Jennifer Ashton will face charges of assault, and attempted murder against the two of us. She will go to jail, and in the meantime we will have a lot of time to discover the evidence needed to prove she killed Elizabeth Dalton. When you know who to look at, evidence collection becomes much simpler."

"So basically you used us as bait, is what you're saying?"

"Yes, essentially."

"I'm starting to understand why people want to stab you," I muttered in reply.

"If I had told you, you would not have agreed to come, and it was important that you did."

"And why is that?"

"Because you have faced death. And tell me, Cassie Coburn, did you give up when the woman came at you?"

"No," I replied quietly. "No, I remember thinking I didn't want to die."

"*Exactement.* Now you can re-start your life, knowing that."

"I feel like your methods aren't exactly approved by psychologists," I told her with a small smile. Despite my annoyance at the fact that she'd essentially used me as bait, I couldn't help but realize that she was right. I didn't want to die. And it had been a long time since I'd cared one way or another.

Violet shrugged. "Well, they work."

"Anyway," I told her. "I feel like you should be thanking me, too. After all, I was the one who came up with the idea to set a trap."

"I would have figured it out myself eventually. Because of you, it was done maybe twenty-four hours sooner."

I laughed. "I guess that's the closest I'm going to come to getting credit for this from you."

"It is. But you should be glad. After all, you have helped me to catch a murderer. As a doctor, you save lives. That is what I do as well. We have saved lives here, today. It is likely that Jennifer Ashton would have killed again, eventually. The lives are less tangible than those you save as a doctor, and you will never experience the thanks of a family that has seen their loved one saved directly by you, but you have done it all the same."

I nodded. "That is true. I hadn't thought of that."

Just then DCI Williams came in through the door. He looked haggard, and yet triumphant. Like a man who had finally completed a marathon in a personal best time.

"Well?" Violet asked as soon as he walked in.

"She's admitted to everything. She also wants you arrested for assault, but obviously that isn't going to happen."

"Obviously."

"She told us she killed Elizabeth Dalton initially in order to frame her boss, and when that didn't work, thought that she could be the sole blackmailer and drive him out of his job."

"That matches with what she told us as well."

"I have to admit it. You were right about it not being the nephew."

"Of course I was. I was right about all of it."

I chose not to comment about the fact that for a while Violet thought Leonard Browning was the murderer as well.

"Yes, well, as always, we appreciate your help," DCI Williams told her. I had a feeling he would appreciate her help even more if it didn't come with constant disparaging remarks about the incompetence of the Metropolitan police force. His face softened suddenly. "Now, are you all right?"

"Of course I'm all right. I shouldn't even be here. Cassie made the paramedics bring me to the hospital."

"I'm a doctor, you have to do as I say," I replied. DCI Williams smiled.

"I think that's the first time Violet has ever listened to anyone else's advice," he told me. "She must actually like you. Good. It's about time she found herself a friend."

"I do not need friends, I simply used Cassie's expertise as a doctor to help at the beginning of the case," Violet protested, but I couldn't help but notice a bit of color creeping up into her face. I had to admit, even though she was infuriating, arrogant and unpredictable, I kind of liked Violet. I liked her sassy attitude. I liked her complete and total confidence in her abilities. And I liked that she'd seen that I was in trouble and decided to give me a chance. Whether or not she really needed my expertise.

I'd almost been killed today, and yet I already felt like moving to London had been the smartest thing I'd ever done.

* * *

Book 2: Cassie's adventures continue in Bombing in Belgravia.

When an ambassador's children are killed by a deliberate gas explosion, Violet is on the case. But not everything is at it seems. What Cassie expected to be open-and-shut quickly becomes a case of international intrigue and suspicion.

Click or tap here now to read Bombing in Belgravia.

Thank you so much for reading! If you enjoyed Poison in Paddington please help other readers find this book so they can enjoy it, too.

- Sign up for my newsletter here to be the first to find out about new releases: http://www. samanthasilverwrites.com/newsletter
- Check out the next book in this series, Bombing in Belgravia: http://www. samanthasilverwrites.com/bombinginbelgravia

You can also check out any of the other series I write by clicking the links below:

Non-Paranormal Cozy Mysteries

Cassie Coburn Mysteries

Ruby Bay Mysteries

Paranormal Cozy Mysteries

Spellford Cove Mysteries

The Witches Murder Club

Enchanted Enclave Mysteries

Fairy Falls Mysteries

Pacific Cove Myseries

Western Woods Mysteries

Pacific North Witches Mysteries

Pacific Cove Mysteries

Willow Bay Witches Mysteries

Magical Bookshop Mysteries

ABOUT THE AUTHOR

Samantha Silver lives in British Columbia, Canada, along with her husband and a little old doggie named Terra. She loves animals, skiing and of course, writing cozy mysteries.

You can connect with Samantha online here:
Facebook
Email